CHARLIE BUMPERS vs.

THE PUNY PIRATES

CHARLIE BUMPERS VS.
THE PUNY PIRATES

Bill Harley

Illustrated by Adam Gustavson

PEACHTREE
PUBLISHERS

Published by
PEACHTREE PUBLISHERS
1700 Chattahoochee Avenue
Atlanta, Georgia 30318-2112
www.peachtree-online.com

Edited by Vicky Holifield
Design by Nicola Simmonds Carmack
Composition by Adela Pons Atencio

The illustrations were rendered in India ink and watercolor.

Printed in June 2016 in the United States of America by RR Donnelley & Sons in Harrisonburg, VA
10 9 8 7 6 5 4 3 2 1
First Edition

ISBN 978-1-56145-939-1

Cataloging-in-Publication Data is available from the Library of Congress.

To Noah and Dylan—
my inspirations 4 EVAR

Thanks again to my trusted reader Jane Murphy,
and to Nicolette Nordin Heavey and Tiffany Hogan
for their help on the soccer end of things.

Contents

1

The Pirates of Doom

"Charlie Bumpers!" my mom yelled.

"What?" I turned back to the car to look at her. I was in a hurry to get to my first soccer practice with my new team, the Pirates.

"Your water bottle!" she called, holding it out of the car window.

I ran over, grabbed it, and turned to run. I didn't want to be late!

"And your soccer ball," she said.

I ran over and got that, too. "Sec you," I said.

I turned back and ran.

"Wait!" she called again. "Dad will pick you,

Hector, and Tommy up at 5:30."

"Okay," I said.

"You're welcome," she said.

"Thank you!" I yelled back over my shoulder.

I was eager to find my team. It was my first year in the ten-and-under league, and by some miracle, my two best friends, Hector Adélia and Tommy Kasten, were on my team. They were both excellent players. And my mom said that our coach, Mr. Carmody, had been a college soccer coach, so I figured he knew everything.

The Pirates were going to rule the soccer season. We would score a million goals.

Or at least fifty.

Even though we don't keep score in this league.

At least the adults *say* they don't keep score. They say they want us to have fun and work on our skills and not worry about winning and losing.

But I think they *do* keep score. I know I do.

It seemed like there were a thousand kids at the fields behind the high school, all searching for their new teams. I wandered around looking for the Pirates. It was like trying to find one matching pair in a huge drawer of unmatched socks. There was a six-and-under league, an eight-and-under league, and a ten-and-under-league, and this was the first day of practice for all the teams. Finally I spotted Tommy and Hector, walking together.

"Hey, Tommy! Hector!" I yelled.

They both turned and waved.

I jogged over and greeted them with a double high five.

"This year is going to be awesome," Tommy said.

"Can you believe we're all on the same team?"

"The Pirates," Hector said.

"More like the Proud Pirates!" Tommy said.

"The Proud *Punishing* Pirates," I added.

"The three of us together," Tommy said solemnly, raising his hand, "will be known as the Pirates of Doom. Arrrrr!"

"Stupific!" I said. "Stupific" is a word Tommy and I made up that means stupendous and terrific all mixed together.

"We're on Field 4, over there," Hector said, pointing to a far corner of the field. We trotted over. When we got there, we found some boys playing, but they looked really small.

"This can't be our team," said Tommy. "Maybe your dad got the number wrong, Hector."

"I don't think so," Hector said. "He showed me the number on the letter they sent."

"Hey, look, Charlie." Tommy nodded toward one of the boys. "There's Trevor. You know, that little guy from your class?"

"Trevor?"

I couldn't believe it. Trevor never even played soccer at recess. What was he doing there?

4

We stared at the kids running around on the field. One was bouncing a soccer ball with his hand like he was on a basketball court. Another boy was holding a phone and looked like he was playing a game. One kid tried to kick the ball and tripped over it. Almost all of them seemed too small for our league. It didn't look like a soccer team. It looked more like a kindergarten gym class.

This couldn't be our team!

I tapped one of the boys on the shoulder. "Is this the Pirates?" I asked him.

"Yeah," he said. "Did you guys just get here? You have to go check in with Mr. Carmody."

"Where is he?" I asked.

"Over there," the boy said, pointing. "The guy with the yellow shirt."

I looked where he was pointing and saw a man standing on the side of the practice field, arms folded, watching everything that was going on.

He looked old. And wiry. He didn't look like a soccer coach. More like a granddad.

He was the coach? I looked at Tommy, then at Hector. They seemed as surprised as I was.

"Uh-oh," I said. "This isn't what I had in mind."

"Me neither," Tommy grumbled.

Hector just shook his head.

2

It's Hard to Play Soccer without Running

We went over to where the man in the yellow shirt was talking with a woman dressed in a warm-up suit and sneakers. They were both holding clipboards.

"Hi," I said to the old wiry guy. "I'm Charlie Bumpers. And this is Tommy and Hector. Is this the Pirates?" I was hoping he'd say no.

"Sure is," he said. "Glad to meet you. I'm Mr. Carmody." His voice was soft and quiet, not like most coaches. Definitely not like Mr. Shuler, our gym teacher. (We call him the Supreme

Intergalactic Commander of Soccer Balls because he never lets us use the gym equipment.) Mr. Shuler has a very loud voice, except when he's whispering something truly scary, like *"Give me the ball, son, before I eat you."*

Mr. Carmody stuck out his hand and I shook it, looking him in the eye like my dad told me to do when I meet someone.

"What position do you like to play?" he asked.

I couldn't help but notice the coach's eyebrows. They were very bushy and moved up and down when he talked. He was bald on top—it looked like all the hair on his head had moved down to just above his eyes.

"Um...forward," I said.

"I figured." He grinned, his eyebrows bobbing up and down. "Most kids do."

Well, of course I liked to play forward! That's where you get to score goals!

The coach shook hands with Tommy and Hector, then blew his whistle. "Okay, Pirates," he said. "Gather 'round." He didn't yell. In fact, I wondered if he *could* yell. Maybe he was too old to yell, or maybe he wore his voice out when he was coaching a college team.

But everyone seemed to hear him. The other kids all ran over and joined us in a circle. I only saw three or four kids I knew—I figured most of the others were from different elementary schools. I recognized Dominic Bucchino, a fifth grader from our school. He was the biggest kid on the team. But I knew he wasn't very fast.

"Okay, team," Mr. Carmody said, "listen up." He nodded toward the woman with the clipboard. "This is Mrs. Patel. She's Vijay's mom, and she'll be our assistant coach. She knows a lot about soccer, so I'm glad she's here to help."

One kid looked down at his shoes, and I guessed he was Vijay. He seemed a little embarrassed about having his mom there. I guess if my mom were there,

I'd be a little embarrassed, too. Or my dad, since he doesn't know much about soccer. He knows a lot about numbers, though, because he's an accountant.

Mr. Carmody had us play a game to learn each other's names. First he had each kid shout out his name and asked the rest of us to yell the name back, until we'd gone around the whole circle. Then we took turns calling out the name of someone in the circle and kicking the ball to him. After a while I knew just about everyone's name. Then the coaches set up a line of orange cones and showed us how to practice dribbling the ball around them.

I looked over at Tommy and Hector. We all shrugged. Great big duh! Doesn't everyone on a ten-and-under team know how to dribble a soccer ball?

I guess not. Some kids didn't have a clue how to dribble. Mr. Carmody had to demonstrate how to kick the ball lightly with the side of your foot.

Then they paired us off so we could practice passing the ball back and forth.

While I was waiting for Mr. Carmody to assign me a partner, Trevor David came over and said hi.

"I didn't know you liked soccer," I said. He was known in our class as the dinosaur king. He knew everything about dinosaurs. It was all he ever talked about. I'd never even seen him kick a soccer ball.

"I don't really like sports, but my dad says I need the exercise," he grumbled. "So my parents signed me up."

"Oh," I said.

"I don't like running," he said.

Hmmm, I thought. *It's hard to play soccer without running.*

I was hoping I'd get paired with Tommy or Hector, but I saw that they'd already been put with other kids.

"Charlie Bumpers," called Mr. Carmody. "Victor Swann. You two are partners."

Victor seemed like a nice kid, but I could see right away that he wasn't a very good soccer player.

The first time I passed the ball to him, it skittered through his legs. He lumbered after it, picked it up with his hands, and brought it back to where he started. Then he took a step back and gave it a big kick, sending it bouncing off in the wrong direction. I ran after the ball, dribbled it back, and passed it to him again.

The same thing happened.

"Just kick it back easy, like this." I showed him.

"Okay," he said.

He gave it a little nudge with his toe, and it rolled a few feet and stopped. Next to me, Hector was passing a ball back and forth to a kid named Oliver Cardenas, who was as skinny as a stick and about the size of a second grader. Hector passed it perfectly. But instead of stopping the ball with his foot, Oliver booted it. The ball flew over Hector's head and smacked into Mr. Carmody's rear end. I thought the coach might get mad at Oliver, but he just rolled it back to Hector.

It seemed like a lot of kids had never played soccer before. Other than Hector, Tommy, and me, I only saw a couple of other kids who seemed to know what they were doing. Vijay, for one. And Danny, Mr. Carmody's son, looked pretty good.

After the drills, the coaches divided us into two teams, seven on a side, so we could play a practice game—a scrimmage. Finally! The Pirates of Doom could show everyone some real soccer.

But Tommy and Hector were on the other side.

"Charlie," Mr. Carmody said, looking at his clipboard, "I'd like you to play goalkeeper."

My mouth dropped open.

Not goalkeeper! I didn't want to stand around the entire game and hope nobody kicked the ball at my head. I wanted to be a forward where I'd get to score goals!

Boogers.

3

A Big Blob of Plasma

The scrimmage started and I watched from the goal. I could see that the Pirates had a big problem. When you play soccer you're supposed to stay in your position. If you're a defender, you don't run up toward the opponent's goal. If you're a forward or striker, you don't run all the way back to your own goal. That was how you were supposed to play.

But not the Pirates.

Almost everybody except Hector, Tommy, Danny, and Vijay ran everywhere, or ran away from the ball when it came near them. Hank, Billy, and Jeremy ran around in circles, pushing and stumbling.

The ball went back and forth in the middle of the field, with most of the kids bunched up together like a big blob of plasma floating in space. Sometimes they tried to kick the ball, but mostly they kicked each other. Even the good players couldn't get a play going.

Mr. Carmody blew his whistle and reminded everyone to stay in position. But when we started playing again, the floating blob of soccer players formed just like before.

I noticed Victor and Oliver standing off to one side. They were on opposite teams, but they were both looking at Victor's cell phone.

"Victor!" I yelled. "Get back on defense!"

He didn't hear me.

I wandered out a little farther from the net and yelled at him again.

Just then the ball squirted out of the big pile of kids. Hector got it and dribbled it down the side. I ran out to meet him, but he centered it toward the middle of the field. I turned around too fast, stumbled, and fell on my face. As I lay on the ground, I saw Tommy kick the ball into the net.

Goal.

"Charlie," Mr. Carmody said. "You were too far out."

"Sorry, Charlie," Tommy said.

Boogers. Again.

At the end of the scrimmage, Mr. Carmody had us run around the soccer field. Twice.

Trevor just walked the second time around.

Then the coach gathered us in a circle again.

"Good practice today," he said. "A lot of you played hard and I like to see that. But we have to play smart, too. You saw what happened when everyone was all bunched up and the goalkeeper wasn't in the net. It was easy to score."

Mr. Carmody didn't look at me, but I could feel my ears turning red. It was Victor's fault for playing with his phone!

"And I don't want you bringing anything to practice that doesn't have to do with soccer. No games. No toys. No phones. For an hour and a half, it's just us and a soccer ball. Do you understand?"

I looked at Victor and Oliver. They were bobbing their heads up and down like they would never do such a thing.

"Now," he went on, "we're going to hand out the jerseys. You'll get a red one and a blue one. Each week we'll wear one color or the other, depending on if we're the home team. On the schedule it lists the color you should wear. Make sure you bring the right one."

Mrs. Patel gave us our jerseys and game schedules.

The shirts were fresh and new, and I couldn't wait to wear one in a game. The blue one was the best. Across the front was our team name—PIRATES— in bright white letters. On the back was a number.

I got number 7, which everyone says is lucky.

"We only have a few practices before our first game against the Tigers," Mr. Carmody said. "Try not to miss any of them. Our games are on Saturdays at nine. I'd like you here at 8:30 so we can warm up. Everybody will play at least half the game each time, and I'll be trying you out in different positions. You'll all get a chance to play everywhere."

I was glad I'd already had my turn at goalkeeper.

"And finally, in a couple of weeks, we'll be handing out boxes of chocolate bars to sell for the league. We really need everyone to pitch in so the league can buy new equipment and pay the refs. Mrs. Patel will be in charge of keeping track of the sales. So start thinking about who might buy some candy from you. See you all at practice next Thursday."

Selling stuff! Oh no! Grown-ups are always having kids sell things. In second grade I had to sell greeting cards and wrapping paper for a school fundraiser, and it had been a complete disaster. Nobody on my street wanted to buy anything, and my mom only bought one roll of wrapping paper with candy canes on it because she felt sorry for me. I sold the least in my class, and of course Samantha Grunsky, who is ALWAYS in my class and ALWAYS ANNOYING, sold the most in the whole school and won a bicycle.

Eating candy bars is a wonderful idea. Selling them is not.

As practice finished, Dad pulled up in our car. Tommy, Hector, and I climbed in the backseat. My older brother Matt was in the front seat, holding a video camera. Matt was in middle school. He was always watching movies, and now he had joined an after-school video club. All of a sudden he had started acting like a famous director, taking videos of everything. He especially liked filming me. I knew he was doing it just to bug me. Once he followed me into the bathroom. That made me really mad.

As soon as we climbed in the car, my brother turned his camera on us.

"Stop it," I said.

"Barbarians in captivity," he said in a science-show-narrator's voice. "Never recorded before on film. See how primitive they truly are."

Hector smiled.

Tommy grunted and moaned like a caveman.

I rolled my eyes.

◆ ◆ ◆

That night at dinner, Mom ladled out chili from the stove and brought the bowls to the table. As soon as she set down my bowl, Matt focused his camera on me and began narrating. "This is rare footage of a *Bumpers idioticus* feeding in its natural habitat. Notice how widely it opens its mouth when it takes—"

"Stop it, Matt!" I said.

"That's enough, Matt," Dad said.

"I'm just doing research!" my brother protested. "We're supposed to make a documentary about something strange."

"I mean it," Dad said. "No devices at the table other than our arms and our heads."

"What about our stomachs?" my little sister Mabel asked. Dad calls her Squirt, but I call her the Squid. It's funnier. "You have to have your stomach if you're eating."

"Okay," Dad said. "Stomachs are allowed."

"And our throats," the Squid added.

"That, too," Dad agreed. "Okay, Squirt. You go first. What happened to you today?"

"Well..." The Squid took a deep breath like she was going to talk forever. Which she did. She went on and on about how Mrs. Diaz, her first-grade teacher, had gone on a whale-watching trip, and then she hadn't seen any whales, and then it rained every day, and then...and then...and then...

Finally she finished.

"Charlie?" my dad said. "You want to tell us about soccer practice?"

"I saw Charlie's team from the car when we picked him up. They're mostly little guys," Matt observed. "If they're pirates, they're the Puny Pirates."

"Matt, stop it," Mom said. "It's Charlie's turn. What did you do in practice?"

I glared at Matt. "Well, um, we did a bunch of different drills," I said. "Then we played a scrimmage."

"What position did you play?" Mom asked.

I frowned. "Goalkeeper."

"Really?" Mom asked. "How did you like it?"

"It stunk. I had to stand around the whole time and Tommy and Hector were on the other side."

"Did you let in any goals?" Matt had this very annoying habit of knowing the exact wrong question to ask.

"One."

"Who scored it?" Matt was like a shark who smelled blood in the water, closing in for the kill.

"Tommy," I mumbled.

"Your best friend?" Matt asked, evil in his voice.

"Okay," Dad interrupted. "What about your day, Matt?"

"Well," said Matt, "my big news is that my future as one of the world's great movie directors has been destroyed by my parents, who won't let me film when I need to."

"That is truly horrible," Dad said, smiling.

Matt rolled his eyes like only a twelve-year-old brother can.

4

A Human Zoo of Soccer

On the Saturday morning of our first game, I woke up really early with butterflies in my stomach. I was nervous, but I couldn't wait to get to the field.

When I dress for a soccer game, I have a very particular method, which I invented last year. First, I put on my shorts (well, after my underwear, *great big duh!*), then I spread my shirt out smoothly on the bed with the front side facing down and the bottom of the shirt hanging just off the edge. I put the shirt on by wriggling my arms and head in at the same time.

Next comes my left shin guard, then my right. I put on my left sock, then my right, and pull them all the way up over the shin guards. After that I put on my shoes, first the left one, then the right. The last thing I do is tie each lace, left then right, with a double knot.

The first time I used my special method, I scored two goals. I've dressed that way ever since.

It doesn't always work.

But I still do it.

I dressed perfectly that morning. This was an excellent sign! Then I hunted for my soccer ball, which I finally found in the car. I started to dribble around the backyard, practicing going back and forth between my left and right foot. (I'm right-footed, so left foot is harder.) I kicked it a couple of times against the garage, very gently.

Dad immediately stuck his head out the back door. "Don't kick that ball against the garage," he reminded me. How had he heard those tiny little kicks?

"Don't let Ginger out!" I yelled, but it was too late. She leapt off the steps, barking all the way across the yard. I guess she had heard the kicks, too. She hated the soccer ball—almost as much as she hated her sworn enemies, cats and squirrels.

Ginger tried to bite the ball like always, which was impossible since it was way bigger than her mouth. I dribbled the ball around the yard, trying to keep it away from her. She never gave up. Dad finally called her back into the house and told me to get in the car.

By the time we got to the soccer field, there were already tons of kids in red and blue and green and yellow jerseys running around. Soccer balls were flying all over the place. Parents stood on the sidelines blabbing to each other. It was a human zoo of soccer.

I found our team. Hector was already there, dribbling the ball up and down the field. He kicked it to me and we started passing it back and forth. Tommy showed up, and pretty soon the three of us were running up and down the field. We kept passing the ball to each other until one of us kicked it in the goal, then we did it again.

"Goooooooaaal!" we would all yell together. "The Pirates of Doom rule! Arrrrr!"

"I wonder how many goals we'll score," I said after a few runs down the field. "Maybe ten?"

"Fifty," Tommy said. "Most definitely fifty."

Hector just shrugged his shoulders and smiled.

Of the three of us, Hector is the quiet one. Tommy and I are loudmouths, but for some reason, Hector doesn't seem to mind.

Mr. Carmody called the Pirates over and gave us a talk. "Remember what we've been working on during practices, boys. Stay in position. Make good passes—nothing more than ten yards, except for the two defenders. And don't get too far out on the sides with the ball. If we keep ourselves in the middle of the field, we'll control the game. And when you're in a contest for the ball, don't be afraid to go after it. Controlling the ball means we control the game."

I looked across the field at the Tigers. Yikes. They were all a lot bigger than we were, and they laughed and joked and kicked the ball to each other like they thought they were superstars or something. I recognized Jaden Craig and Jack Browning, two fifth graders from our school. It seemed like all the Tigers were fifth graders. We only had two kids that old on our team, Dominic Bucchino and Jeremy Moradian, and Jeremy wasn't that big.

Mr. Carmody told us who would start and where.

I was a midfielder with Billy Berman.

Hector was a forward with Sebastian Salgado.

Tommy was on the sidelines.

There was no way we were going to score fifty goals like this! The Pirates of Doom needed to be on the field at the same time.

But at least I wasn't goalkeeper.

The ref blew the whistle and the Tigers started things off. Right away one of them kicked it all the way down the field. Oliver swung his foot at the ball but missed it completely. When Thad Matthews, our goalkeeper that day, ran out to get the ball, it bounced off his chest. It rolled right to one of the Tigers, who kicked it straight into the net.

Twenty seconds. One to nothing, Tigers.

After that it just got worse.

They scored another goal.

And then another.

The Tigers were eating us alive.

Mr. Carmody kept shuttling players in and out. Tommy, Hector, and I—the Pirates of Doom—were never all on the field at the same time. Once, Hector made a beautiful pass to Dominic, who boomed it really hard toward the goal, but their gigantic goalkeeper punched it way back out onto the field.

Another time, Trevor was between our goal and Jaden Craig, who was dribbling the ball right toward him. Instead of trying to stop him, Trevor put his hands on his head and ran the other way, screaming like he was being attacked by a bear. Or maybe a tyrannosaurus.

A lot of adults were yelling, including the coach from the other team. But Mr. Carmody hardly raised his voice, except to call in substitutions.

At halftime, the score was 4–0. I knew, because I was keeping score in my head.

"We stink!" Tommy said, eating one of the orange slices Mrs. Patel was handing out.

"I know," I muttered.

But Mr. Carmody didn't seem bothered. "Listen,

everyone," he said, "your job this half is to always know where the ball is, even if it's nowhere near you. Defenders, don't run past the midline. Don't bunch up. We made some good plays. Let's have fun and try to shut them down this half."

"These teams are not fair!" Cody Dillon complained.

Mr. Carmody didn't say anything. As we started the second half, I saw that Mom had showed up with Matt and the Squid. Matt already had his camera pointed toward the field.

"Score a goal, Charlie!" the Squid yelled.

Mr. Carmody had put me in as a defender, so I wasn't going to score a goal. I couldn't explain that to the Squid.

The second half wasn't much better. The Tigers scored three more goals. I stayed back pretty far and every time I got the ball, I stopped, looked, and then passed it to someone up the field.

A couple of times a Tiger bumped me out of the way. Both times I looked at the ref, who was a high-school kid, to see if he would call a foul, but he never did. Was he blind? Couldn't he see these guys were huge giants pushing us around like we were little elves?

Right before the game ended, the Tigers made a mistake. One of their players tried to pass it back to their goalkeeper and it went in their own goal.

So we scored. Kind of.

The ref blew the whistle. The game was over. We all lined up and shook hands.

"Eight to one," some kid said to me.

"*Seven* to one," I shot back.

"Whatever," he said.

I was beginning to think not keeping score was a really good idea.

5

Traffic Jam

In school on Monday, Hector, Tommy, and I sat together at our regular lunch table and moaned about losing.

"No one else got beat that bad on Saturday," Tommy said.

"We weren't very good," Hector said.

"Not very good? We were terrible," I said.

"What are we going to do?" Tommy asked.

"Play better," Hector answered.

"Duh!" I said, but I knew he was right.

"How can we play better?" Tommy asked. "Mr. Carmody won't put us in together. And half the kids on our team don't even know what they're doing."

We were all quiet for a few minutes, concentrating on our meatloaf and Tater Tots.

"I have a question," said Hector suddenly. "Tell me again why we have to sell candy bars?"

"To raise money for the team, I guess," Tommy said. "It's not so bad. If you sell enough, you can win a prize."

"Yeah," I agreed. "But that's not likely. The last time I had to sell something, it was a disaster."

"I remember that," Tommy said. "I did okay that year because my aunt and uncle bought $50 worth of greeting cards."

"I've never had to sell anything."

"Welcome to America, Hector," I told him. "Where adults send kids out to sell things."

"It could be worse," Tommy said. "You could work for my dad."

"What do you mean?" I asked. "Your dad has the greatest job ever."

I would have loved to work for Tommy's dad. He was the parks and rec director, in charge of taking care of all the playing fields and basketball courts and playgrounds in town, which sounded great to me. "I wouldn't mind cutting the grass riding on one of those huge mowers."

"Yeah, that part's okay," Tommy said. "But my dad's also in charge of the dog parks."

"So?"

"If you're a new worker, your first job is going around every day and cleaning up the dog parks."

"So?" I asked again.

"The dog parks? Get it? Cleaning the *dog* parks?"

Hector and I looked at each other in horror. "Oh no!" we said at the same time.

Tommy just nodded. Hector shook his head.

"I have to pick up Ginger's poop every day," I said. "But imagine picking up after one hundred dogs."

"See what I mean?" Tommy said.

"Okay, cleaning up the dog park is worse than selling stuff," I admitted.

Right then, Jaden Craig and Jack Browning, the

two fifth graders on the Tigers, showed up at our table. They had big smiles on their faces.

"You guys stunk on Saturday," Jaden said.

I looked at Tommy. His eyes were shifting back and forth and he was biting his bottom lip, which meant he was thinking about saying something. He has a habit of blurting things out before he thinks, and sometimes it's the VERY wrong thing. I hoped he would keep his mouth shut this time.

"We scored more goals for you than you did!" Jack added. "Maybe you should play in the eight-and-under league."

Jaden laughed out loud.

"Oh, yeah?" Tommy said.

Jack glared at him and grunted, "Yeah."

"Just wait until next time," Tommy said. "We'll destroy you."

Hector and I opened our mouths, but no words came out. We stared at Tommy like he was a moron space being from a Buck Meson television special.

"Destroy us?" Jaden asked. "Are you serious?"

"Definitely! We're called the Pirates, but me, Hector, and Charlie are known as the Pirates of Doom. Arrrrr! Right, guys?" Tommy looked at us for support.

Our mouths were still open. What was he thinking?

"Um, sure," I said.

Hector just took off his glasses and rubbed them on his shirt, which is what he always does when he's nervous.

"You guys are so dead," Jaden said. "I can't wait to tell the other guys on our team." The two Tigers walked away laughing.

"Are you insane?" I asked Tommy. "They're going to kill us!"

"I know," he said. "Are you going to eat the rest of your Tater Tots?"

◆ ◆ ◆

That week at practice, Mr. Carmody started us off with a new drill.

"Dribbling is an art," he said. "You have to kick

the ball far enough ahead so you can run,
but if the ball gets too far in front of you,
someone else will steal it." He gave us each
a ball and had us line up along the sides of
a big square he had marked off with plastic
cones. "Okay, guys," he said. "This drill is
called Traffic Jam. When I blow the whistle,
you will all dribble across the square at the
same time to the other side, then back.
Keep it under control. We'll start off slowly
at first."

It was a perfect traffic jam of soccer
balls.

Practically everyone kicked their balls
into the middle and immediately started
pushing each other out of the way. Dominic
kicked any ball he could find and booted it
out of the square. Victor tripped and sat in
the middle of the square, his arms covering
his head so he wouldn't get hit. Trevor

dribbled around the edges of the square, avoiding everyone. Three or four of us were dribbling back and forth like we were supposed to, but most of the other kids were running all over the place chasing a ball someone else had kicked.

We were not the Powerful Pirates. We were not the Punishing Pirates.

Like Matt said, we were the Puny Pirates, our own worst enemies! No one had to beat us. We beat ourselves.

Finally Mr. Carmody blew the whistle. "We have some work to do," he said, shaking his head.

During our scrimmage, I got to play forward, but Tommy was defenseman, and the coach put Hector in the other goal.

When practice was over, Tommy went up to the coach. "Mr. Carmody," he said, "you should let Charlie and me and Hector play on the same side. We'd score a million goals."

"A million?" Mr. Carmody asked, raising his eyebrows.

"Most definitely," Tommy said. "Or at least a thousand."

"I'll keep that in mind," Mr. Carmody said.

When grown-ups say that, it usually means that they plan to forget about it right away.

There was one piece of good news, I guess. Mrs. Patel told us that the candy bars hadn't been delivered yet, so we were saved from the horror of selling things for at least another week.

6

Boom-Boom

I would like to tell you that we won our second game. But we didn't. We lost to the Sharks four to nothing. I know. I kept score.

That was bad, but the third game was even worse. It wasn't even close.

The Cougars scored twelve goals. I think. It's hard to keep count when someone scores that many times.

It was really easy to keep track of how many times we scored, though.

Zero. None. *Nada*, as Hector says.

I played midfielder for the first part of the game. Then Tommy came in and I went out. Like I expected, Mr. Carmody had forgotten that Tommy, Hector, and I—the Pirates of Doom—could score a thousand goals together.

Near the end of the game, Mr. Carmody called his son and Dominic over. I was standing on the sidelines watching. "Danny and Dominic," he said, "I'm putting you into the backfield. Just clear the ball out of there as far as you can. Don't get far away from the goal."

The boys nodded.

Mr. Carmody looked at Dominic, waggled his eyebrows, and smiled. "Show them your big foot, Boom-Boom."

When Dominic heard what the coach had called him, he smiled. Right then, I knew Dominic had a new name. Boom-Boom.

By that point there was no way we could catch up with the Cougars. Still, Danny and Dominic managed to get the ball all the way down the field a bunch of times. And we only let the Cougars score one more goal.

At the end of the game we had to shake hands with the other team. A couple of the Cougar players laughed at us. It didn't feel good at all. Mr. Carmody shook hands with the other coach but didn't say anything. Then he called us over and told us to sit down. We were all tired and disappointed. It hadn't been any fun.

"That was a hard game," Mr. Carmody said.

"The teams aren't fair," Cody whined, repeating his usual complaint. "And the same two big guys made nearly all the goals."

"You're right," Mr. Carmody said. "Most of you guys are fourth graders, and most of them were fifth graders. But this is the team we have, and I'm happy with it." He looked around the circle. "How many people here never played on a soccer team before this year?"

Five kids raised their hands.

"How many of you didn't know what a goal kick was at our first practice?"

Six kids raised their hands.

"How many know what a goal kick is now?"

Everybody raised their hands.

"How many people know what the different positions are now?"

We all raised our hands again.

"Well, we know a lot more than we did at the beginning of the season," he said. "And we're playing better. But what I'm most proud of is how you didn't give up. None of you stopped. Don't worry, we'll be fine. See you at practice on Tuesday."

I wasn't thinking about scoring fifty goals anymore. Now, I just wanted to win a game. Any game.

Halfway through our practice the next Tuesday, a girl showed up. Mr. Carmody introduced her as Tess Salgado. Sebastian told us she was his sister and said she was an eighth grader. "She plays for the middle-school girls soccer team. That's why she still has her soccer clothes on. She's really good."

Tess helped Mr. Carmody and Mrs. Patel with the drills, and they even let her be the referee during the scrimmage.

Just as practice ended, Dad pulled up and honked the horn. Hector, Tommy, and I said goodbye to everyone and ran over to the car. Matt was in the front seat, camera in his hand. But for once he wasn't filming us. He was staring out the window at the field.

"Hey, guys. Isn't that Tess Salgado?" Matt asked.

"Yeah," I said. "She's Sebastian's sister."

"Oh," Matt said. I was expecting him to make fun of us about something (anything!), but he didn't, which was a minor miracle, since teasing me was his main occupation. Instead he just looked out the window at Tess.

What was that about?

7

Chocolate Bars for Sale!

I don't want to talk about the next game. Except to say it was against the Raiders, a team that hadn't won a game either. But now they have, thanks to us.

We did score one goal that day. Vijay stole the ball from someone right in front of the other team's goal and kicked it in. We all went crazy. Tommy put a hand over his eye like an eye patch and yelled, "Arrrrr!"

"Arrrrr!" we all yelled back, like real pirates.

Then we gave up six goals in ten minutes.

After practice the following Tuesday, Mr. Carmody told us we were improving every week.

But everything still felt the same to me.

While Coach Carmody was winding up his talk, Mrs. Patel went over to her car with Vijay and they brought back two big cartons. "Chocolate bars for sale!" she called. We all gathered around as she opened the first carton.

It was filled with boxes. Boxes of big chocolate candy bars. More chocolate candy bars than I'd ever seen.

She handed a box of twenty to every boy on the team. Then she gave each of us a sheet for keeping track of what we sold and an envelope for the money.

"The candy bars sell for two dollars each," she said. "When you sell a candy bar, mark it down on the sheet. If you sell the whole box, you should have $40. If you have sold all your candy bars and want to sell more, you can turn in your money and

ask me for another box. And remember, the boy who sells the most bars gets a new soccer ball, a professional jersey, and a warm-up jacket."

I was glad Samantha Grunsky wasn't on our soccer team. She'd be sure to win. And then tell me all about it.

Mr. Kasten, Tommy's dad, was waiting for us when practice was over, so we all climbed into the backseat of his car.

"I can't believe I have all these candy bars," Tommy said.

"Neither can I," Hector said.

"Neither can I," Tommy's dad said.

"It seems cruel that we have them and can't eat them," I added.

"We could eat some," Tommy suggested.

"You have to pay for them first," Tommy's dad said as he drove down the street.

Tommy screwed up his face and rolled his eyes. Sometimes you forget that parents in the front seat are listening to everything you say.

"Candy bars will be easier to sell than greeting cards," I said.

"Or working for my dad," Tommy whispered. "Dog poop!"

Hector and I nodded.

"What was that?" Mr. Kasten asked, looking at us in the rearview mirror.

"Nothing," Tommy muttered.

That night Mom and Dad said they would each buy two candy bars. That meant I had already sold four! After dinner, I went into my room to do my homework. The first thing I saw was the box of candy bars sitting on my desk. I took one out of the box. It was as big as any candy bar I'd ever gotten on Halloween. I could smell the chocolate through the paper. I looked in my desk drawer for money and found a dollar. Maybe I could sell myself half a candy bar.

The Squid stuck her head in the door.

"What are you doing?" she asked.

"Nothing."

She took a step into the room. "What are you doing with that candy bar? Are you going to eat it?"

"No," I said.

"If you do, could I have a bite?" she asked.

I thought about it. Maybe if I shared the candy bar, it would make things all right. "Do you have any money?" I asked her.

"I have a quarter."

That made it even better. "Okay," I said, "go get it."

"Wait! Don't open it yet." She ran out the door and came back a split second later holding up the quarter. "Here it is," she said.

I put my dollar and her quarter in the big envelope, then I very carefully took the paper off the candy bar. It was

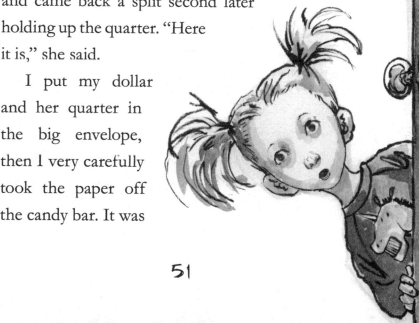

marked into eight pieces, so I broke off one square for the Squid. "Here. One quarter buys an eighth of the candy bar."

"That's not very much," she said. "I only get eight quarters for my allowance and I already spent one of them."

I knew I couldn't explain fractions to her, so I broke off another little square and gave it to her. "There," I said. "That's more than your share."

The door opened and Matt's video camera appeared. "Here is the prehistoric animal in his room," said the science-show-narrator's voice, "with his younger sibling—" He switched back to his regular voice. "Hey, are you guys eating the chocolate that Charlie's supposed to be selling?"

"I paid for it," the Squid told him. "A whole quarter."

Suddenly Matt was no longer a snotty, movie-making brother. Now he was a friendly, kind, best buddy. "What about sharing with your older brother?"

"You have to buy one if you want to eat it," I said.

"Come on," Matt said. "I'll pay you later."

My brother was famous for telling me things that weren't exactly true. "Show me the money," I said.

"Tomorrow, I swear. Cross my heart, hope to die."

"You hope you'll die?" the Squid asked.

"It's just a saying," Matt explained.

"It's a bad saying," the Squid announced.

"You know I'm good for it, Charlie," Matt argued. "Everybody else in the family is eating your chocolate. Why not me?"

"Okay, but promise," I said, handing him a candy bar.

"When have I ever not kept my word?" Matt asked.

"What about the time you said you'd give me a piggyback ride all the way from the beach to the house but then you didn't because it was too far?" the Squid asked.

"Yeah," I added. "And what about the time on vacation you told me I could sit by the window if I gave you my onion rings, but then you wouldn't move?"

"Those don't count," Matt explained. "But this does. I promise as your older and smarter brother, I'll pay you."

I gave him the candy bar. He tore away the paper, broke off a huge piece, and stuffed it in his mouth.

Now I had sold six candy bars.

But I had only collected one dollar and twenty-five cents.

◆ ◆ ◆

Sunday afternoon, I picked up the box of candy bars and headed out the door to try and sell them on my street. I went from house to house, knocking on doors and ringing doorbells, hoping someone would want to buy something.

No one was at home at the first six houses. At one place the babysitter answered the door and said she didn't have any money. The cat lady (her two cats tease Ginger every time we walk by) was getting in her car and told me she didn't have time. I don't think she liked me anyway after what happened that time her cats jumped out the window. I couldn't help it that Ginger barked at them and tried to leap into their house.

I came to the Gritzbachs' house. They're kind of old but my parents are friends with them. Mr. Gritzbach is especially grumpy and doesn't like Ginger. I knocked, hoping his wife would answer, but he opened the door.

"Um, hi, Mr. Gritzbach," I said.

"Hello," he grumbled.

"Would you like to buy a candy bar to support my soccer league?" I asked. "They're only two dollars."

"I'm allergic to chocolate," he growled.

"Thanks any—"

"You're welcome," he said, shutting the door on me.

Who could be allergic to chocolate? Only Mr. Gritzbach.

Mrs. Lapidus, who lives on the other side of the block, wanted to buy some, but she only had a five-dollar bill. "Is there a special deal if I buy more than one?" she asked.

"I guess so," I said, and gave her three bars for five dollars.

A whole hour selling candy bars. I'd only sold three. And I was short a dollar.

Boogers.

◆ ◆ ◆

When Tommy and I got off the bus Monday morning, Hector was waiting for us.

"I tried selling candy bars yesterday and it didn't

go well," he said. "Some people didn't answer the door. Two ladies told me that they never bought things from door-to-door salesmen. One guy just looked at me and shut the door in my face. It was no fun."

"I know what you mean," I said. "I didn't have much luck either." We looked at Tommy.

"I haven't tried yet," he said. "But I think my parents will buy some."

"I don't like selling things," Hector said. "It makes me nervous."

I thought for a minute. If I had to sell candy to strangers in Chile, I'd probably be nervous, too. "What if you, Tommy, and I sold candy together?" I suggested. "Even if it didn't work, at least we could have a good time."

"Stupific idea!" Tommy said. "We could go door to door in each of our neighborhoods!"

"As long as we don't go to the Gritzbachs' or the cat lady's house," I said.

Hector grinned. "I like this plan."

"Okay. Hector, ask your parents if you can come home with Charlie and me on the bus Wednesday afternoon," said Tommy. "We can start in my neighborhood. We'll sell a million."

"Or at least a hundred," I said.

8

Pure Genius

At recess, the three of us met by the fence. "If only Mr. Carmody would let us play offense together," Tommy said, "we could score more."

"Look." I searched around, found a small stick, and got down on my knees. "Let's make up a play we can show Mr. Carmody. Then he'll see that the Pirates of Doom should play together."

I drew a diagram of a soccer field in the dirt. I put little circles for Hector and Tommy as forwards and one for me as a midfielder. "I have the ball and kick it here," I told them. "Then you go here, Tommy, and you go over here, Hector." I drew lines to show where we would go and who had the ball.

"That is brilliant," said Hector.

"Exactly!" Tommy agreed. "The Pirates of Doom will conquer all."

"Forget conquering," I said. "I just want to win one game."

◆ ◆ ◆

While everybody was doing their quiet reading in class, I got out some paper and a pencil and drew out the soccer play again. I made a couple of changes to the one I'd drawn in the dirt. At the top I wrote *What do you think of this?* and passed it to Hector.

He looked at it, got out a pencil, and began to mark on it. I leaned over to see what he was doing. "Wait a minute," I said, pointing. "What if I ran here?"

Now our play was even better!

One problem.

I'd forgotten about our teacher, Mrs. Burke, who as far as I can tell is not interested in soccer at all. She and I'd had some trouble at the beginning of the year, but now I like her. And she likes me, I think. Once she said to me, "Charlie, you and I have an understanding."

That means she understands the way I am, and I understand the way she is. So she's not surprised when I have a hard time staying in my seat, or my desk is messy, or I lose an assignment.

It also means that I understand her class is Mrs. Burke's Empire. She is the Supreme Ruler and I am her servant.

POW!

One giant finger snap rang out, blistering my ears. It was Mrs. Burke, snapping the loudest fingers on the planet. They're like the fireworks finale on the Fourth of July.

"Charlie and Hector, are you reading?"

Trick question! No good answer!

I picked up a book and pretended to read. Then I looked over at Hector. His ears were red. I knew he was embarrassed. He never gets in trouble.

When Mrs. Burke stopped at Sam Marchand's

desk to ask him something, I reached for the diagram.

POW!

Exploding fingers again!

Mrs. Burke walked back to us and picked up the paper. "What is this?"

Hector didn't say anything. He was looking at the floor, which must have been pretty interesting, because he kept staring at it.

"It's a soccer play," I said. "We're on the same team and we have to make up some plays."

"Put this away, Charlie. I don't want to see it for the rest of the reading period."

I folded it and slipped it in my desk.

Boogers.

◆ ◆ ◆

On the bus that afternoon, I showed Tommy the changes Hector and I had made to the play. He was so excited he started bouncing his leg up and down.

"This is pure genius!" he crowed. "I like how you run around and then I move toward the side. Look here—when Hector runs behind me, it looks like he's making the shape of a banana!"

"That's it!" I shouted. "We'll call the play the Banana!"

Tommy switched into his announcer voice: "Adélia on the left, Bumpers up the middle. Kasten with the ball to Bumpers, moving behind him. Adélia around Kasten. Adélia open! Watch out! It's the BANANA! Goal! Goal! Goooooaaal!" He stood up and pumped his arm, put his hand over his eye and yelled, "Arrrrr!"

"Hey!" Mr. Tutman, the bus driver, glared at us in the rearview mirror. "Keep it down!"

Tommy dropped back into his seat. We looked at each other, bumped fists, and shouted at the same time.

"BANANA!"

"I mean it!" Mr. Tutman bellowed.

◆ ◆ ◆

I was going to take the play to practice and show Mr. Carmody, but I forgot and left the paper at home. Tommy and I tried to explain it to him before our first drill started.

"It's called the Banana," I said.

I explained that when I got the ball I'd pass to Hector, who'd be on my left. Then Tommy chimed in and told him about Hector running in a circle behind us. We took turns telling about the whole play. It took a long time, and Mr. Carmody just kind of stood there with a weird look on his face, his bushy eyebrows moving up and down.

"And then the Pirates of Doom score," Tommy said at the end.

"The Pirates of Doom?" Mr. Carmody asked.

"Uh, yeah. That's us," I explained. "Tommy and Hector and me."

Mr. Carmody nodded. "We'll see," he said. Then he blew his whistle and called everybody together.

"That didn't work," I told Tommy.

"Maybe it did," Tommy said. "He didn't say no."

"We'll see is the same as no. My dad says it all the time."

"No, it's not," Tommy said confidently. "Only no is no. We'll see is maybe, which is halfway to yes."

"We'll see," I said.

"Listen up, everyone," Mr. Carmody said, spinning a soccer ball in his hand. "Some of you have been asking about heading the ball. We don't let you guys do that until you get older. Your brains are still developing, and so that has to wait. But you can still use other parts of your body." He gave the ball to Mrs. Patel. "For instance, you can use your chest to trap the ball like this."

Mrs. Patel tossed the ball at Mr. Carmody. He raised his chest and the ball hit it and dropped right in front of him. "If you practice this, you can stop the ball when it comes at you, then be ready to go the other way. Let's pair off and try it. Throw it easily to your partner so they have a good chance to trap it."

My partner was Trevor. When I tossed the ball at him, he stuck out his chest and closed his eyes. The ball hit him in square in the face.

"I'm not doing chest traps," he said, rubbing his nose. "They're too dangerous."

"Good idea," I said. "Let me try."

He heaved the ball and I watched as it sailed way over my head.

9

Goooooaaa!

We lost our next game to the Sharks, but they didn't blow us out. Maybe if Mr. Carmody had let the Pirates of Doom join forces, we would have won. Or at least scored, which we didn't.

All I wanted to do now was win one game.

And get rid of the candy bars.

The next game was against the Raiders again. I showed up Saturday morning thinking we might have a chance of winning for a change. Hector and Tommy and I had practiced the Banana every day at recess. I had carefully dressed the exact right way. I'd even remembered my water bottle.

At the field, Mr. Carmody gave us our positions:

Hector and Danny were forwards, Vijay and I were midfielders, and Dominic and Trevor were defenders. Billy was in the goal.

The Pirates of Doom were still not together!

"Yellow Bomb, boys," Mr. Carmody told us. We all nodded. That was the name of a play we'd learned from Mr. Carmody and practiced over and over again. It was for the beginning of the game or after a score.

The Yellow Bomb was almost as excellent as the Banana. But starting with this play meant the ball would come to me right away. My heart started thumping like crazy.

"Charlie," Tess Salgado said.

"Yeah?"

"When Hector passes you the ball, don't hurry. Stop it, take your time, and take a step back so you kick it really well."

I nodded. She talked like she knew I could do it, and just hearing her voice calmed me down a little. The starters went to the center of the field for the beginning of the game. Hector positioned himself in the center circle, ready to pass the ball as soon as the ref blew the whistle. I stood a little behind him, to his right. Hector gave me one of his little smiles, adjusted his glasses, and then looked away. I knew he was ready. I was, too.

Phweeeeet! The whistle sounded.

Hector passed the ball to me. I stopped it, took a step back, and then kicked it as hard as I could toward the left corner.

Danny streaked down that side of the field, and the ball landed right in front of him. He reached the ball before the defender knew what was happening and stopped it. Danny spotted Hector running down the field, so he tapped it in his direction. Hector got the ball on the run, then dribbled toward the goal. When Hector gave a little head fake, the goalkeeper ran that way and Hector kicked the ball in.

Goal! Goal! Goooooaaal!

We all screamed and ran up to Hector. Danny tackled him and I jumped on top.

Tommy yelled "Arrrrr!" then ran onto the field and dived into the middle of us.

We were ahead! For the first time in the season we were ahead!

Even if we weren't keeping score.

Mr. Carmody actually clapped his hands and smiled. Our parents all cheered. All the Pirates were happy. We were not puny! Or piddling! Or putrid! Or paralyzed!

Then the Raiders scored.

Three times.

In a row.

The third goal was the worst. The ball was loose and it rolled near Victor. I ran over to help him—I could tell by looking that he didn't plan to be anywhere near the ball.

"Kick it, Victor!" his dad yelled.

Before I could get there, Victor stumbled over and gave the ball a big kick!

Right into our goal.

"Not that way!" his dad yelled.

I looked at my dad. He was standing with the Squid and had his hands in his pockets. I was kind of glad he wasn't yelling, even if he wasn't cheering, either.

Matt was filming the game. I noticed that he'd worked his way around the sideline until he was standing close to Tess.

Somehow, thinking that we'd actually had a chance at winning made losing feel even worse. At the end of the game, Mr. Carmody gathered us all around. We hadn't won, but he didn't seem very upset. "That was the best we've played this year," he said.

I guess he was right. We only lost by four goals. But it still didn't feel good.

"We passed well," he said. "We made some mistakes on defense, but we also kept the ball out of our end most of the time. Over the weekend, I want every one of you to practice dribbling and passing. Find something you can use as a backboard and practice hitting a target. We'll see you Tuesday."

"And don't forget to bring your candy money," Mrs. Patel said.

Hector and I walked toward the parking lot together. Hector's dad was going to take all of us to his house for lunch, and then we were going to sell candy bars together. When Hector and I were climbing in the car, Tommy came running up with two more cartons of candy bars.

"Look what I got!" he said.

"More candy? Why?" Hector asked.

"Well, I told Mrs. Patel we needed more because we've already sold a lot," Tommy said. "At first she told me no more boxes until we turned in the money for the ones we sold. But then I explained how we were going to work together this afternoon in Hector's neighborhood and really needed more candy bars right now. So she gave them to me. I had to promise to bring the money on Tuesday."

"Wow," I said. "That's a lot of candy bars!"

"I know," Tommy said. "It's a catastrophe of candy bars."

"I don't think you're using the word right," I told him.

But it turned out he was right. It *was* going to be a catastrophe.

10

That's Why I Hate Him!

After our lunch, we started around Hector's neighborhood, still dressed in our soccer uniforms.

We all took turns talking. I was in charge of knocking on the doors, saying, "Hello, we're from the youth soccer league," and introducing us. Tommy was in charge of telling people how good the candy bars were and how much they cost. Hector was in charge of saying thank you, since he was the most polite one in our group.

In an hour we had sold fifteen candy bars and collected $33. A lady who'd bought one bar had given us a five-dollar bill and told us to keep the change.

"This is great!" Tommy chortled. "We almost sold a whole box!"

"We're going to win the prize!" I hooted.

"It's too bad we don't get a goal every time we sell a candy bar." Tommy reached in the box and pulled one out. "I think this deserves a reward!"

"I do, too!" I reached in and took out two more bars. I handed one to Hector. "Let's celebrate."

"I don't know, you guys." Hector stared at the bar in his hand. "We have to pay for every one we eat."

"We'll be okay," Tommy said. "We're already three dollars ahead. If just one more person gives us five dollars instead of two, then we'll almost be even. Come on, Hector. Just this once!"

"Okay," he said. We sat down on the front step of Hector's house and started to eat the candy bars.

"Oh man!" Tommy closed his eyes in ecstasy. "I'm dying, this is so good. It's the best chocolate I've ever had in my entire life."

"I know," I said. "And you know what else? We

are the best candy-selling team ever. It worked great to divide up the talking."

"Right," agreed Hector. "It's much, much easier when we do the job together."

"Hey," I said. "What if we shared by each taking a part?"

"What do you mean?" Hector asked.

"Well, each of us would do a different thing. Hector, you're good at keeping track of stuff. Maybe you could be in charge of marking down the candy bars we sell and how much money we collect."

"Okay," he said.

"Excellent plan, Charlie," Tommy said. "Maybe you should hold the money."

"Okay," I said.

"And I'll keep the candy bars," Tommy added.

"Perfect!"

"But we should each keep some candy bars to sell," Hector said. "Just in case."

"Stupific!" Tommy and I shouted at the same time.

The three of us bumped fists. The Pirates of Doom worked so well together, for a minute I forgot we'd never won a game.

◆ ◆ ◆

Matt always spent a lot of time in his room with the door closed, but lately he'd been shutting himself up in there more than usual. It made me wonder what was going on.

Right before dinnertime, I went upstairs and put my ear to his door. I tapped on the door, but he didn't answer. I knocked again. "Matt. Hey, Matt!" Still no answer.

It's almost always a dumb idea to bother my brother when his door is closed. He can get really mad. But I was really curious.

I opened the door very quietly. Matt was sitting at his desk with his headphones on, doing something on his computer.

I snuck up behind him to see what he was doing.

He was looking at a video…

Of our soccer team!

It was a scene of us letting in a goal! Then there was one of me letting the ball go through my legs. The next one showed me getting pushed out of the way by one of the Tigers.

"What are you doing?"

Matt yelped and nearly fell out of his chair. "What are you doing in my room?" he shouted, tearing off his headphones.

"What are *you* doing with that stupid video?" I shouted back.

"Get out!"

"Stop making movies about me!" I screeched. "You're making fun of me and the Pirates!"

"No, I'm not!"

"Yes, you are! You're a stupid bozo!"

I was so mad, I didn't even care if Mom heard me call him stupid, which I'm not supposed to do. I tried to push him, but he grabbed both of my arms and shoved me out the door and closed it behind me. I pounded on the door. "Stop it!" I yelled. I didn't want to cry. If I did, Matt would tease me and make things even worse.

The Squid came out of her room. "What's happening?"

"I hate Matt!" I yelled.

"You're not supposed to hate him," the Squid said. "He's your brother."

"That's why I hate him!" I said.

I heard my father's footsteps. When he got to the top of the stairs, he stopped and stared at me.

I tried to wipe off the tears and the snot coming out of my nose.

"What's going on, Charlie?" Dad asked.

"Matt's making fun of me and my team," I said. "He's making a video about how bad we are."

Dad frowned. "I'll talk to him, Charlie. Go help

your mother with dinner."

"I don't want to help," I said.

"Go," he ordered. "Squirt, you too."

"But I didn't do anything," she said.

"I know, but go downstairs and help Mom."

I started down the stairs. I heard Dad knock on the door.

"Matt, open up," he said.

"I'm busy," Matt called.

"No, you're not," Dad said.

I turned back to see what would happen.

"Downstairs, Charlie," Dad warned. "Now."

Boogers.

When it was dinnertime, Matt came down with Dad. We sat around the table. No one spoke. I folded my arms and glared at Matt. He folded his arms and glared at me.

"Matt?" Dad said.

Matt rolled his eyes and looked at the ceiling. Then he muttered, "I'm sorry."

The Squid looked at me. "Now *you* say okay, Charlie."

"I don't like you making fun of me and my team," I said to Matt.

"Okay, I know," Matt said. "Trust me."

I rolled my eyes.

"And I don't like you coming in my room," he added.

"Sorry," I said. Although I didn't really mean it.

"Now everybody's sorry and it's okay," the Squid announced.

But it wasn't.

"Don't forget," I said to Matt. "You still owe me two dollars for the candy bar!"

11

A Math Moron

The next Wednesday after school, I waited around for Mom to get home. She was going to take me over to Tommy's house, where we were all meeting to sell candy bars. After I'd walked Ginger, I went out in the driveway and practiced kicking my soccer ball. Ginger kept chasing it and pushing it with her nose, trying to bite it. Once she clamped her teeth on the bottom of my pants and pulled on them. If Ginger played for the Puny Pirates, the other team would never score.

We quit our weird soccer drill when Mom showed up. I ran into the house and got the big envelope with all the money in it and the candy bars I hadn't sold yet. Mom drove me to Tommy's, where I saw

Hector and Tommy waiting in the yard. I hopped out of the car.

"You're welcome!" Mom called.

"Thank you!" I called back.

I held the envelope up to Tommy and Hector. "Here's the money," I said. "And I brought the candy I have left over."

"The other candy bars are in my room," Tommy said. "I already put Hector's candy in with it."

"I've got the number sheet here," Hector said. "Let's go figure things out."

We went into Tommy's room and sat on the floor. Hector looked at the sheet. "According to my records, Mrs. Patel gave us a total of one hundred candy bars, twenty each on the first day, and then the forty she gave Tommy on Saturday. That means if we sold them all, we would have $200."

"Wow!" I said. "I'm pretty sure we don't have that much."

"I collected some money, too." Tommy pulled a wad of wrinkled bills from his drawer and dumped them on the floor.

"Let's see how it works out." I poured all my money onto the floor alongside Tommy's pile. There were a few coins, a five, and a twenty, but it was mostly one dollar bills. We counted it up.

"We have $78.25," Hector said, writing it down on the paper.

"I still owe $2.75 from the bars my brother and sister ate," I said.

"And we ate three that day when we sold them in my neighborhood," Hector said. "That's another six dollars we should have."

"This is really complicated." Tommy scratched his head like he didn't get it at all.

I did the figuring in my head, like my dad taught me. "That means we should still have $113 worth of candy bars."

"Okay," said Hector. "Then we should have fifty-six candy bars."

"Where are they, Tommy? We need to count them."

Tommy got the box and dumped the candy out on the floor.

I could see right away there were not fifty-six candy bars. We counted. Twice.

There were only twenty-nine.

"That's impossible," Hector said. "We're missing twenty-seven candy bars?"

"Where are they?" I asked.

"Right here," Tommy said. "That's how many we have."

"But it doesn't add up," Hector said. "We have to sell fifty-six more bars to get up to $200!"

"Okay," Tommy confessed. "I ate some. I should have told you guys. I couldn't help it. And I gave a bar to my sister Carla. And one to my cousin. He said he'd pay me."

"How many did you eat?" I asked.

"I don't know exactly," he said. "I wrote it down, but I can't find the piece of paper."

"You must have eaten at least fifteen or twenty," I said.

"I don't think I ate twenty," he said. "That seems like a lot."

"You have to pay for the ones you ate," I reminded him.

"I know!" Tommy said. "That's why I asked for more. This way, we'll sell all those new ones and get the money back."

I looked at Hector. He had his hands over his face like he'd been watching *The Shrieking Skull*.

"Look, Tommy," I said, trying not to panic. "We can't make our money back by selling more candy bars."

"Why not? Can't we just sell more until we get even?"

"No!"

"Why not?" Tommy asked again.

"Because you have to pay for each bar, even if you eat it. If we got new ones, we would owe that much more money. If we're missing $60 now, then we'd always be missing $60. Even if we sold another 100 candy bars."

"But that would be 200 more dollars!" Tommy said. "Then we could pay it back."

"Noooooooo!" I wailed. My best friend was a math moron! "That $200 would only pay for the new candy bars."

"But..." Then Tommy's eyes opened wide. His mouth opened wide. "Oh!" he said. "Now I get it."

"You're a bozo!" I said.

Hector was shaking his head.

"It's not my fault they tasted so good," Tommy reasoned.

The more we tried to figure things out, the more

confused we got. All we knew was that we'd only collected $78.25 and we owed Mrs. Patel $200.

"Are you sure we shouldn't just get more candy bars?" Tommy asked.

"No more candy bars!" Hector warned.

"Maybe we could sell the bars we have left for five dollars each instead of two," I suggested.

"I don't think anyone would pay five dollars," Hector said.

"I wouldn't," Tommy said. "I mean, they're really good, but…"

We sat on the floor of Tommy's room, looking at the piles of money and candy bars.

"Maybe our parents will lend us the money," Hector said.

"My mom will kill me," Tommy said. "When I told her I was in charge of all the candy bars she said it was an accident waiting to happen."

"Two hundred dollars," I moaned. "I think I'm going to throw up."

"Want a candy bar?" Tommy asked.

12

Only Me to Stop It

The following Saturday was our next-to-last game. We were playing the Cougars, who had beat us twelve to nothing.

Even though no one was keeping score.

I really wanted to win a game, but beating the Cougars seemed pretty doubtful.

I needed to change our luck. While I was laying out my clothes, I decided to switch around the order I got dressed in. I was getting desperate. I wasn't sure what I was going to say when Mrs. Patel asked us about the candy bars and the money. If I told her what was really happening, she might have a heart attack or something.

I thought about telling my mom, but I wasn't ready to hear a lecture.

I am never ready to hear a lecture.

Changing the way I got dressed must have brought me at least some good luck. There was so much going on before the game, nobody even mentioned the candy bars. For once it was the grown-ups who forgot what they were supposed to be doing.

Mr. Carmody announced that he was putting Dominic and Hector in the backfield to defend. Tommy was in midfield. Victor and Oliver would be forwards, which was pretty weird. There was no way they could ever score a goal.

"Let's see how you two guys do up there," Mr. Carmody said, his eyebrows bobbing. "You've got great hands, Charlie. Take the net for the first half."

The net? I really didn't want to be goalkeeper, and I really didn't understand why he would put Victor and Oliver up front.

I wanted to protest, but before I could open my mouth, Cody Dillon started begging to be put in as a forward. "Please, Mr. Carmody," he wailed. "I've never gotten to be a forward!"

"We'll see," our coach answered. After that I decided to keep my mouth shut. I didn't want to sound all whiny like Cody. And besides, Mr. Carmody had told me I had great hands.

Tess brought me a yellow goalkeeper jersey. I put it on and took my position in the goal. She stood nearby for a couple of minutes, giving me some tips.

"Don't just move your hands and arms, Charlie," Tess said. "Move your whole body toward the ball. Move your feet first, okay?"

I nodded.

"And you're the field manager," she went on. "You have to tell Hector and Dominic what players are open on the other team. And call out their names when you throw them the ball. You're in charge!"

"Okay," I said.

That was a lot to remember. Playing goalkeeper was turning out to be a lot harder than I thought.

For the first five minutes of the game, no one scored. We almost never had the ball in their end, because whenever Victor or Oliver got it, the Cougars just took it away from them.

I yelled every time I saw someone open on the other team, just like Tess had told me. Dominic and Hector would run to cover the position. Whenever I got the ball (which was a lot), I looked for someone on our team, called out their name, and threw them the ball. I don't know how many shots I stopped. It seemed like a million.

Or at least fifty.

Coach Carmody kept telling us to stay in the center, close to our goal. He seemed excited that the Cougars hadn't scored on us yet. Once, their biggest guy kicked the ball, and I dove at the last minute and pushed it out of bounds.

A lot of people cheered.

It wasn't as much fun as scoring, but it wasn't bad.

On the next inbound pass, Dominic stole the ball and gave it a big boot.

"Boom-Boom! Boom-Boom!" we all chanted.

The ball sailed up in the air and far down the field, toward the other team's goal. Everybody took off after it. Everybody.

Even Dominic and Hector.

"Hector!" I shouted. "Position!"

But Hector, the fastest kid on our team, saw a chance to score. He raced on down the field. Oliver and Victor were dancing and hopping around in the middle of the field like cheerleaders, yelling "Go, Hector!" Tommy reached the ball first and made a perfect pass to Hector, who took it in stride in front of the goal and kicked it.

It flew right toward the net, but their goalkeeper leapt into the air and snagged it with both hands.

All the Pirates and their parents groaned.

Everyone on our team stopped running.

And before I knew it, the Cougars goalkeeper had rolled the ball out to one of his teammates, who turned and kicked it down the right side of the field.

Trevor was on that side at midfield.

"Trevor!" I yelled. "Ball!"

Trevor woke up from whatever dinosaur dream he was having. He saw the ball bouncing toward him and started to run for it. It was the first time I'd ever seen him run, but it was too late. One of the forwards on the other team took it and dribbled it right by him.

Tommy, Dominic, and Hector were behind, running as fast as they could to catch up. It was a breakaway toward our goal, with only me to stop it.

I ran out in front of the goal to try and cut down the angle on their forward. Before I could get very far out, he took aim and kicked the ball. Really hard.

Right at me.

It smashed into my stomach so hard it knocked me to the ground and bounced out of my arms.

I couldn't breathe for a second. I saw stars and heard people screaming. The ball was lying right beside me and I tried to reach for it, but one of the Cougars kicked it into the empty goal.

I was still trying to get my breath when Coach Carmody and Mrs. Patel came running out on the field. Mr. Carmody helped me up.

The Cougars were cheering and jumping on each other.

"Are you okay, Charlie?" Mr. Carmody asked, his arm around me.

I nodded, but my eyes were filling with tears. It didn't seem fair that I had stopped the ball and gotten knocked over and they had still scored. I was having a really hard time breathing.

"Substitution," Mr. Carmody said to the ref. "Sebastian, you take over at goal."

Hector came up to me. "Charlie, are you all right?" I could tell by the look on his face that he felt horrible.

I nodded.

"I'm really sorry," he said. "I shouldn't have run up there. I'm sorry, Mr. Carmody."

"It's okay, Hector," I said. "We almost scored."

Mr. Carmody gave Hector a pat on the shoulder and walked me off the field. Mom was standing there waiting for me and so was the Squid, holding Ginger on the leash. Ginger jumped on me when I reached them.

"Are you okay, honey?" Mom asked. I could tell she was worried.

"Yeah," I said. I kind of wanted a hug from her, but at the same time, I kind of didn't.

"It wasn't nice of that boy to kick the ball in your stomach," the Squid said. "He should get a time-out!"

Mr. Carmody knelt down in front of me and held my shoulders and looked me right in the eyes.

"Charlie, that was a perfect play on your part. You did exactly what you were supposed to do. Nobody could have done it better."

"But they scored," I said.

"Big deal," he said, like it didn't matter at all. "What matters is how you played. And you played great."

Wow. My stomach hurt, but I felt good.

Late in the game I went back in as a midfielder. The Cougars were ahead, five to nothing. Just before time was up, I passed the ball to Hector and instead of heading to the goal he kicked it across the field to Danny, who put it in the net. Their goalkeeper was completely fooled.

When the game ended, Mr. Carmody gathered us around like he always did. "That was our best game yet," he said. "I'm really proud of the way everyone played today." It felt good to hear him say that, but it was hard to forget everything that had happened, and that we still hadn't won a game.

In the car, Matt said, "I got it all with my camera. This is great cinematic drama! I got a spectacular shot of you writhing on the ground in pain!"

I just looked out the window and counted up the season score.

So far we were losing something like 45 to 3.

13

My Brain! It's Exploding!

On Sunday afternoon, Tommy and Hector came over to my house. We all went up into my room and closed the door.

"I don't think we'll ever win a game," I moaned. "We only have one left, and there's no way we'll beat the Tigers."

"I thought we played better last Saturday," Hector said.

"I saw Jaden in the hallway on Friday," said Tommy. "He was bragging about how they haven't lost a single game this season. I told him we were going to crush them."

"Tommy!" I said. Hector just shook his head.

"I know, I know. But I just got sick of him talking trash all the time."

"We might as well get used to their bragging," I said. "If they beat us, they'll have a perfect season. And we'll have a perfect season, too. A perfect *losing* season."

"Forget about that," said Hector. "Today we need to worry about the candy money."

Tommy had brought the candy bars and Hector had the numbers sheets. I took the envelope from my desk drawer and dumped the money onto the floor.

"According to my sheet," Hector said, "we have collected $78.25. Not counting the quarter, that means we still owe $122."

"And here's the eight dollars my mom and dad owed us," I said, dropping the bills onto the money pile. "Now we have $86 and we only owe Mrs. Patel...um...$114."

"Ugh!" Tommy put his hands over his eyes. "This is like a problem on a math test! I hate tests!"

"Here," I said, "give me the pencil and paper." I wrote it out as I talked. "We have twenty-nine candy bars left. If we sell them all, that will make another $58. But then we'll still be $56 short of the total we owe to Mrs. Patel."

Tommy clutched his head. "Aaaaah! My brain! It's exploding!"

"Wait!" I said. "I got five dollars for my allowance last week. And I'll get five more this week. That's ten dollars. "

"I have some money saved, too," Hector said. "I think I have fourteen dollars."

Tommy frowned. "I've got nine dollars. I was saving it for our trip to Fun World, but…"

"Come on, Tommy. You're the one who ate so many, remember?" I said.

"Okay, okay. I'll put in my nine dollars."

"I think we'll still be short!" I said.

Hector took the pencil back and did the adding and subtracting again. "That means if we sell all the candy bars we will still need $81."

"I guess," I said. Now I was getting confused, too. "How did you get that number?"

Hector looked at the sheet. "I'm not really sure," he confessed.

"Okay." Tommy frowned. "Let's just say we need a lot more money. Like a hundred dollars."

"Maybe somebody will pay a little more for the candy bars," I said.

"Not my parents," Tommy said. "They already bought three from me at the regular price. They said they weren't buying any more."

"My parents bought some already, too," I said.

"So did mine," Hector added.

"We've hit all our neighborhoods. Who else could we sell to?" I asked.

"Wait!" Tommy said. "I know!"

"Who?" Hector and I asked at the same time.

Tommy gave us one of his sneaky smiles. "Teachers," he said. "Teachers love chocolate."

Sell the candy bars to teachers. What a stupific idea.

14

We're Going to Be Rich

Before practice on Tuesday, I took out the envelope with all our candy money. I added the five dollars from last week's allowance and the five from this week. On the outside of the envelope I wrote our names. Tommy and Hector were bringing their money, too, and I would add it in. I just hoped it would be enough to satisfy Mrs. Patel for now. We'd have to promise to bring her the rest on Thursday. However much that was.

But Mrs. Patel wasn't at practice!

I was relieved, because I wouldn't have to explain everything. Tommy had forgotten his money, but Hector added his $14 to the envelope. I didn't have a pencil to change the total, but I handed the money over to Mr. Carmody and told him that we would turn in the rest on Thursday.

However much that was.

"All right," he said. "Just don't forget to tell Mrs. Patel on Thursday."

Now we just had to sell the rest of our candy bars on Wednesday. And beat the Tigers on Saturday.

We were either the Pirates of Doom, or the Doomed Pirates.

At dinner that night, the Squid talked about her first piano lesson.

"And I know where middle C is," she said. "Charlie and Matt, do you know where middle C is?"

"It's in the middle," Matt offered.

"That's right," said the Squid. "Mrs. Fernthaler showed me how to play it with my thumb."

"I can play 'Chopsticks,'" Matt said. "And also 'Smoke on the Water' on the electric guitar, if I had one."

"What about you, Charlie?" Mom asked. "How was soccer practice?"

"Practices are fine," I said. "It's the games that stink."

"As long as you're having fun," Mom said.

"Playing is fun. Losing is not."

"You said they don't keep score," the Squid said. "If there's no score, you don't lose."

"Or win," Matt added. "Luckily, I have it all documented for posterity."

"What's that mean?" the Squid asked.

"Keeping it for the future—when Charlie has kids and he can show them how great his team was."

"Matt," Dad warned.

"I mean it!" Matt said.

"Ha ha ha!" I said. And didn't mean it.

"No one in this house believes anything I say!" Matt complained.

"Charlie, how are the candy bar sales going?" Mom asked.

"Um, okay." I did not want to talk about candy bars with my mother.

"Have you been keeping track? Do you have many more to sell?"

"Um, yeah," I muttered. "We're going to sell some more tomorrow."

"I bet you've been eating them," Matt said.

"You still owe me two dollars!" I said.

"I'm a little concerned, Charlie," Mom said. "Isn't it complicated keeping track of all that money and all these candy bars? Do you need some help?"

Uh-oh. I looked at my plate and everyone got quiet.

"I'm sure Charlie's okay," Dad said, smiling at me. "He can figure out everything with Tommy and Hector, right?"

"Uh-huh," I said. At least Dad trusted me.

Even though maybe he shouldn't have.

"Okay," Mom said, "but let us know if we can help."

I was counting on the teachers to help. That's their job, isn't it?

◆ ◆ ◆

On Wednesday, Tommy, Hector, and I finished our lunches early and headed for the teachers' lounge. We got to the door and looked up at it. It was closed.

"I don't know if we're allowed to go in there," Hector said.

"I was in there once," Tommy said. "They have a machine where you can buy water and juice drinks. And a copy machine."

I'd never been inside the teachers' lounge. We looked at the door again.

"Someone knock," Tommy said.

"Not me," said Hector.

Just then, the door opened and Mr. Romano, my third-grade teacher, came out. "Hey, you troublemakers," he said. "What are you doing here?"

"We're trying to sell candy bars for our soccer team," I said. "They cost two dollars each. We wanted to ask the teachers."

Mr. Romano took out his wallet and pulled out two dollars. "I'll take one. Come on in and ask the other teachers."

"Thanks!" I said.

We walked in the room. There were six or seven teachers sitting around a table. I was a little nervous, but I calmed down when I started telling them about our soccer team and the candy sales. I also explained if they really wanted to help, they could give us three dollars for a bar instead of two. Hector nodded. Then Tommy showed how good the candy bars were by opening one, tasting it, and collapsing on the floor in delight. The teachers loved it. Hector collected the money and thanked the teachers. Tommy handed out the candy bars. Mrs. Burke

bought two candy bars, but she gave us ten dollars and said to keep the change.

What a great teacher!

We were doing really well. Then Mrs. Rotelli, our principal, showed up.

"I don't really want you boys selling candy in school," she said. "It's not fair to the other kids. You should head back to your classes."

Mrs. Rotelli didn't know how desperate we were. But at least she let us keep the money. Mrs. Burke offered to hold the money and the rest of the candy until the end of the day. I figured the Teacher of the Year was trustworthy.

After school, she gave me back the candy and the money.

"Be careful, Charlie," she said. "You'd better put the envelope in your backpack."

On the bus, I handed the box of candy bars back to Tommy. "Count them, but don't eat any!"

"We got rid of twelve more bars," he said. "How much money did we get?"

I took the envelope out of the backpack and counted the bills.

"There's $40 here," I said. "We sold twelve candy bars, and with the extra from Mrs. Burke we made $40!"

"We're going to be rich!" Tommy said. "Maybe we should each have a candy bar to celebrate!"

"No!" I said.

"Just kidding."

We still had a way to go, but it seemed like things might work out. Walking home from the bus stop with the Squid, I started thinking that our luck was finally turning around.

15

BOOGERS!

That night after dinner I opened my backpack to take out my books. I wanted to put the candy money in my desk drawer so I wouldn't lose it.

I looked through the big pocket.

No envelope.

Then the smaller pocket.

No envelope.

Then the side pockets…

NO ENVELOPE!

The money was gone!

BOOGERS!

I ran downstairs and looked around the kitchen to see if it had fallen out. Then I put on my jacket and pushed open the back door.

"Where are you going?" the Squid asked.

I didn't answer. Even though it was getting dark, I walked up the street toward the bus stop, looking to see if I had dropped the envelope somehow. There was no sign of it.

I tried to think. The last place I'd had it was on the bus, when Tommy and I were counting the money. I must not have put it back in my pack.

I left it on the bus.

I got this horrible feeling in the bottom of my stomach, like I had swallowed a radioactive alien that was eating my liver.

"Stupid, stupid, stupid!" I said to myself. "Bozo, bozo, bozo, bozo!"

When I came in the back door, the Squid asked me where I'd been.

"Nowhere." I went straight up the stairs and headed toward my

room. But then I turned around and knocked on Matt's door. He didn't answer.

I pounded harder.

"Busy!" he shouted.

I opened the door. When he saw me, he closed his computer. I sat down on his bed, put my head in my hands, and started moaning.

"What's wrong?"

"I lost the money we made today selling candy bars."

"You lost it? What a moron!"

"I know!"

"Where'd you lose it?"

"I think I left it on the bus this afternoon."

"Uh-oh," Matt said.

"What?"

"High-school kids are the first ones on that bus in the morning. They'll find the money. You'll never get it back."

"Oh no! What am I going to do?"

"You could ask Mom and Dad to loan you the money," he suggested.

"They'd kill me!" I said. "Matt, you've got to help me."

"You're going to have to figure out a way to make some quick money. Maybe Hector or Tommy will have an idea."

"I'm going to die."

My brother reached into his desk and took out three dollars. "Here's what I owe you, plus one extra."

"Why didn't you pay me earlier?" I asked.

"You didn't need it then," he said. "But you need it now."

16

Kicking Poison Soccer Balls at My Head

I asked our bus driver Mrs. Lima if she'd found an envelope on the bus.

"No, Charlie," she said. "If anybody found it, it would be your afternoon driver, Mr. Tutman."

Or the high-school kids, I thought.

Tommy got on the bus and plopped down on the seat next to me. "Hey!" he said.

"Hi," I answered back.

He saw right away that something was wrong. "What's the matter?"

"Everything!" I said.

"No, it's not!" he said, smacking me on the back. "We only need to make a little more money to pay for the candy bars. And I think we're going to destroy the Tigers."

He saw he wasn't making me any happier. "What is it?"

I looked at the floor, then out the window, then up at the ceiling.

"What? Did somebody die?"

"Not yet," I said, "but maybe soon. I lost the money."

"WHAT?" he yelled, standing up. Everybody on the bus turned and looked at us.

"I must have left it on the bus yesterday afternoon after we counted it."

Tommy immediately stuck his head under the seat to look.

"It's not there," I said. "I bet some high-school kid got it. They ride this bus, too."

Tommy put his hands on his face and pulled back his cheeks. "Aaaaaaaaaah! We're gonna die!"

"I know!"

"Even Hector is going to kill us!"

"I know!"

"I hate candy bars!" Tommy shouted.

"Keep it down back there!" Mrs. Lima called.

◆ ◆ ◆

Hector was waiting for us in front of the school. When I told him what I'd done, he said, "You bozo!"

Great. Hector's English was improving, and now he could call me a bozo.

"I know," I said.

"Are you sure you looked everywhere?" he asked.

"Uh-huh," I mumbled.

"We are in very bad trouble," he said.

I nodded. I was a bozo, but at least my friends didn't hate me. They acted like it was a problem we all had.

None of us knew what to do. Today was our last practice of the season, and Mrs. Patel was sure to ask for the money. I was hoping maybe Mr. Tutman had found the envelope, but for some reason that afternoon he wasn't driving the bus.

Maybe he found the money and quit his job.

◆ ◆ ◆

Toward the end of soccer practice, Mr. Carmody gathered us in a circle.

"Saturday is our last game," he said. "I know the team we're playing is very good. And I know that some of us keep score, even though we say we don't. But I want you to know that regardless of what happens, I've seen each of you become a better player this year. If you sign up next year, you can stay on this team. We're going to keep improving. A lot of you will be fifth graders then, and we'll be ready to show who we are."

We all applauded and cheered. "Pi-rates! Pi-rates! Pi-rates!"

"Arrrrr!" Tommy roared, with a hand over one eye.

"Arrrrr!" everyone roared back. "Arrrrr! Arrrrr! Arrrrr!" they chanted.

Mr. Carmody held up a hand for silence. "Now,

on Saturday, we're going to play a defensive game. With old Boom-Boom Bucchino back there as sweeper, we're going to keep the ball away from our goal. We're going to keep it packed in tight. And who knows, maybe one of you will get a breakaway and you'll surprise everyone. Even yourselves. But you won't surprise me.

"Before you go, make sure that Mrs. Patel has all of your money and whatever candy bars you didn't sell."

Uh-oh. I glanced over at Tommy, who looked like he was gagging. Hector was cleaning his glasses.

Mrs. Patel spoke up. "We've all done very well. I don't know about all the other teams, but I doubt that anybody else has sold as many as

we have. Oliver sold eighty-four candy bars!"

Then she paused and looked at Tommy, Hector, and me. "But we need you to turn in all your money and candy bars. Charlie?"

"We'll have it all in on Saturday," I said.

Mrs. Patel sighed. "Do I need to call your parents?"

"No!" we all shouted at the same time.

"Okay," she said, then added, "but don't forget. I know where you live."

While she was collecting money from the other guys, Tommy, Hector, and I stood in a small circle and looked at each other.

Finally Hector spoke up. "What are we going to do?"

"I'm thinking maybe we need to tell our parents," I said.

"Oh no!" Tommy gulped.

"My parents are away until Saturday morning," Hector said. "I have a babysitter staying with me."

"Let's just tell Hector's babysitter," Tommy suggested.

"Seriously, guys," I said. "I don't know what else to do."

"Let's just wait one more day," Tommy said. "Maybe a miracle will happen."

◆ ◆ ◆

I couldn't do my homework that night. I couldn't think straight. I wanted to tell my parents about the problem, but it was even more complicated with Tommy and Hector being involved.

Mom came in just before bedtime and asked me if everything was okay. I almost told her then, but I was still kind of hoping maybe Mr. Tutman, our afternoon bus driver, had found the envelope. I fell asleep thinking about candy bars and money and huge soccer players with the name TIGERS on their jerseys kicking poison soccer balls at my head.

Who needed a nightmare? I was living in one.

17

Waiting for a Lecture

In class Friday morning, Hector said to me, "Charlie, we have to tell Mrs. Patel."

"I know."

"You guys are talking too much," Samantha Grunsky complained. She sits behind me and is completely annoying.

"We have to talk," I said.

"No, you don't."

"Yes, we do!"

POW! Mrs. Burke's fingers snapped.

"Boys," she said. "You have work to do."

I made a face at Samantha. *That was Samantha's fault. Why doesn't she ever get caught?*

"Charlie," Mrs. Burke said. I looked up. She motioned for me to come to her desk. I walked down the aisle toward her. What now?

"What's up with you this morning?" she asked.

I shook my head. "Nothing."

She led me out into the hallway, then stuck her head back through the door. "I've got my eye on you, class," she said. Then she closed the door.

"What's up?" she asked.

"Nothing," I said.

"You're going to have to do better than that. You've been moping around here for the last two days, and you're not usually like that."

I really, really did not want to tell her what had happened. She was the one who had told me to keep the money in the backpack so I wouldn't lose it. I'd even lost her ten dollars!

But my mouth blurted out what I was thinking. "I lost the money from the candy bars!"

"Oh, goodness." She rested her chin on her fist. "What happened?"

"Tommy and I were counting it on the bus," I said. "We wanted to see how much we had collected. And I guess I didn't put the envelope back in my pack."

I was waiting for her to say "I told you so." I was waiting for a lecture. I was waiting for something horrible.

"You must be very upset," she said softly. "Have you told your parents?"

"No. They're going to kill me."

"Hmmm. I don't think they'll go quite that far."

"They might," I said. "They're always telling me to be careful with my stuff. And now Hector and Tommy and I owe around a hundred dollars and I don't know where we're going to get it!"

"A hundred dollars?"

I couldn't talk. I just nodded.

"Well, that *is* quite a problem. I think you're going to have to tell your parents."

"I was hoping we could just make the money back. We wanted to do it by ourselves."

"I understand that," she said. "But I think you have to tell them."

"Are you going to tell them?"

"No," she said. "That's your job. But I will ask you about it on Monday."

◆ ◆ ◆

That afternoon on the bus, Mr. Tutman told me he hadn't seen the envelope. It made me mad to think someone had just taken it and not turned it in. If I found something like that, I wouldn't keep it. Didn't they know a nine-year-old might die?

Tommy and I could barely talk. I just stared out the window. Tommy got down on the floor to look around again.

"It's not down there," I said.

"Maybe somebody else dropped a $100 bill by mistake."

"And maybe the moon will fall out of the sky," I said.

18

How Do Parents Know This Stuff?

I like soccer. I love soccer.

But some mornings, the bed is so warm and comfortable I could stay there forever. I can't even describe what it feels like. Like rich chocolate milk. Like floating in a lake on a hot day. Like a puffy cloud. Like the burble of the aquarium in the school library. Like—

"Charlie, this is the last time I'm going to tell you to get up!"

Mom was standing in my doorway.

Saturday. The last game of the season. The Tigers. Missing candy bars. One hundred dollars.

Maybe I should stay in bed with the chocolate milk and the clouds and the aquarium.

"Get dressed and come down for breakfast," she said. "We're leaving in fifteen minutes."

I got up and washed my face. "Charlie Bumpers," I said to the person in the mirror, "you are the world's biggest bozo."

I went back in my room and grabbed my soccer clothes. I just put them on as quickly as I could and went downstairs. It didn't look like my specially designed dressing routine was helping anyway.

While I was eating my cereal, miracle of all miracles, Matt appeared. He never got up early on Saturday. He looked like he'd been sleeping in a tornado.

"What are you doing up?" I asked.

"I have an important film assignment. But it's too early for me to talk to anyone, especially you."

"You don't have to come." I really didn't want any more movies being made about me making mistakes.

"I do have to come," he said, filling up his bowl with cereal. "An artist's work is never done. Now don't talk to me."

Dad came in from outside. "Let's go," he said. "The car's running."

"Matt, are you ready?" Mom asked.

He shook his head.

"You take Charlie," Mom said to Dad. "I'll bring Matt and Mabel over before the game starts."

I got my cleats and walked out to the car in my socks. We were pulling out of the driveway when the Squid came running down the steps waving my water bottle.

"Charlie, you forgot this!" She handed it to me through the window. Mom was standing in the door with her arms crossed.

"Thank you," I said out the window.

"You're welcome!" she called as we pulled out of the driveway.

Dad kept his eyes on the street and I looked out the window. It was quiet in the car.

"Thinking about the game?" Dad asked.

I wasn't. I was thinking about the candy bars. And about what Mrs. Burke had said.

"No," I said. I tried to say more but nothing came out.

"Then what?" Dad could tell something was wrong. How do parents know this stuff?

"Dad," I said.

"Yeah?"

"I lost the money for the candy bars."

He just kept watching the road for a minute. Then he asked, "All of it?"

"No," I said. "Forty dollars of it. But we owe a lot more."

"How much?"

"Like $100."

He let out a low whistle. "That's a lot."

"I know."

"You sold that much candy?"

"Not by myself. Tommy, Hector, and I were selling together. But I was in charge of the money.

And we kind of lost track of the candy bars. And we ate some. And now we owe all this money. I put my allowance in, but that didn't help much."

Dad didn't say anything for a long time.

"I don't know what to do."

"I'll help you figure it out," Dad said. "Do Tommy's and Hector's parents know?"

"I don't think so."

Dad didn't say anything after that. I felt bad, but it was good to get it off my chest. I had to admit, confessing hadn't been as terrible as I'd expected. Kids always say "My parents will kill me."

But I was still alive. At least until our game against the Tigers.

◆ ◆ ◆

When we got to the soccer fields, I saw my team warming up. I ran ahead of Dad, holding my water bottle.

"Charlie, you bozo!" Tommy said.

"What?"

"Your shirt!" he said.

I looked at it. It wasn't on backwards or inside out. There wasn't anything spilled on it. I looked back at Tommy. Then I saw the problem.

Everyone else was wearing a red jersey. I was wearing a blue one. The wrong color!

I ran over to Mrs. Patel. "I brought the wrong jersey," I said.

She screwed up her mouth. "Hmmm. Can you get one of your parents to go home for it?"

I looked around and spotted my dad talking to Mr. Kasten. I sprinted over.

"Dad," I said. "I got the wrong shirt. Can you go get my red one?"

He closed his eyes and shook his head. "Maybe Mom hasn't left yet," he said. I stood there while he punched her number on his phone.

"She's not answering," Dad said.

Mr. Carmody called for everyone to gather in a circle. That's when I saw Mom and Matt walking toward us. The Squid was right behind them with

Ginger. When Ginger saw me, she started pulling on the leash and barking.

I ran up to Mom. "I forgot my red shirt, Mom," I said. "Could you please, please, please go get it?"

"Oh, Charlie." She sounded really disappointed.

"Do you want me to go?" Dad asked her.

"No, I'll go." She turned to me. "Where is it, Charlie?"

That was a very good question.

"Umm, I think it's in my shirt drawer."

She headed back toward the car.

"Or maybe in my closet!" I called.

Mom just nodded.

"Or maybe under the bed!"

She kept walking.

19

Arrrrrrrr!

I ran back to the soccer field and joined the team.

"What's with the shirt, Charlie?" called Mr. Carmody.

"My mom went to get my red shirt. She'll be back with it in a few minutes."

He looked at his clipboard. "I had you at forward with Hector. We'll have to start Vijay there instead. Tommy and Victor at midfield. Dominic and Hank in the backfield. Sebastian in the goal. Charlie, we'll get you in when your mom gets back with the shirt."

I couldn't believe it! Coach had finally decided to put Tommy, Hector, and me—the Pirates of

Doom—in together, and I had to pick this day to wear the wrong shirt!

"Okay, team," Mr. Carmody said. "This is our last game. I want you to remember all the things we've practiced. Let's show everyone how much better we've gotten this season. Pirates—hands in!"

We put our hands in. "Arrrrrrrrr!" we all shouted and lifted our hands in the air.

We kicked off, but the Tigers took it away and came running down the field. And there I was, just watching from the sidelines like a bozo.

Victor ran after the ball, but the Tigers forward was big and fast.

"Don't let him get by you, Victor!" his dad yelled.

Dominic poked the ball away from the Tigers player and gave it a big boot down the field. The Pirates fans all cheered.

"Boom-Boom! Boom-Boom!" we chanted.

I could hear Ginger barking over the noise of the crowd.

The same thing happened three more times in

a row. Every time the Tigers got the ball, the same player brought it down the field. And every time Victor managed to slow him down, then Dominic kicked the ball away.

"Positions! Positions!" Mr. Carmody called.

"Go get him, Victor!" his dad yelled. "Run harder!"

It must be pretty annoying having your dad yell at you all the time. I was glad my dad didn't do that.

We weren't able to get the ball into their half of the field very often. Hector got through a couple of times, but there was no one to pass to. Luckily, the Tigers weren't able to score either. Once as they attacked, Hank stopped the ball and kicked it out of bounds.

"Good job, Hank!" his mother screamed.

Just then, Dad yelled, "Hey, Charlie! Mom's on the phone."

I ran over and took it.

"Charlie," Mom said. "I can't find the red jersey."

"Did you look in the closet? On the floor?"

"How could I find anything on your floor? It's a mess!"

This was no time for a lecture! "It has to be there somewhere," I said. "Please hurry!"

"I'll do what I can," she said and hung up.

I got back to the sidelines just as Tommy came off the field. The coach sent Danny in for him.

"Where's your shirt?" Tommy asked.

"Mom can't find it." I guess I looked desperate, because Tommy ripped off his jersey and handed it to me. "Wear this!"

"Are you crazy?" I asked.

"Definitely," he said.

I took off my blue shirt, gave it to Tommy, and pulled his on. "I'm ready," I called, running up to Mr. Carmody. I hoped no one would notice.

"Okay," he said. "We'll put you in for Hector."

Finally I was in the game, but now Hector and Tommy were out. I went in at forward on the right side, with Vijay on the left. We spent most of our time at the center line, watching the Tigers try to kick it in our goal.

Sebastian was doing a good job at goalkeeper. The first half was almost over and nobody had scored. Once, one of the Tigers kicked the ball really hard right at the goal, but it hit the top bar of the goal and bounced back to Dominic.

He booted it down the field.

"Boom-Boom!" everybody yelled.

Coach took Vijay out and sent Oliver in to play forward with me. *There goes our chance to score,* I thought. But it was even worse than I expected. The ref stopped the game twice because Oliver kept drifting too close to the other team's goal. Every time I got the ball, we were offside.

"You have to stay on our side of the other team, Oliver!" I told him.

"Okay," he said. But I don't think he got it.

Coach called me over. "Charlie, you've got to give Tommy his shirt back. I want him at midfield. I'll put you back in when you find a red shirt to wear."

I ran over to the sidelines where Tommy was waiting. I didn't see Mom anywhere. We exchanged shirts again.

Just then, someone tugged on my shorts. It was the Squid.

"Charlie, here!" she said. "This one is red." She pulled off her shirt and held it out.

It had a unicorn on it, but it was red.

It was way too small for me, but it was red.

I gave the Squid my blue jersey and she put it on.

"Let's go, Charlie!" Mr. Carmody called.

I turned the Squid's shirt inside out and squeezed into it. It took a few seconds, but I finally got my hands through the armholes.

"Look at Charlie!" the Squid squealed.

Matt was filming the whole thing with a big, dumb grin on his face. I didn't care. At least now I could play. I ran back out and took my position.

The Tigers took the ball and started down the field. One of the defenders dribbled it right through Oliver's legs. Oliver fell over backwards, sprawled on the grass. He shook his head and got up.

By then, the other Tiger player had passed to a forward running up the center. Sebastian came out of the goal to meet him, and their forward passed the ball off to one of his teammates on the right. Sebastian was out of position, and the forward kicked it right into our goal.

One to nothing.

20

Right in the Rear End

The first half was almost over. I passed the ball to Oliver on the kickoff, but Jaden Craig jumped in front of him, took the ball, and dribbled it down the far side. It looked like he had a clear path to the goal.

Then Boom-Boom appeared out of nowhere. He stepped in front of Jaden and kicked the ball all the way down the side of the field.

"Go get it, Oliver!" I yelled as I ran up the other side. There were only two Tigers in the backfield— a defender and their goalkeeper.

Oliver took off, running as fast as he could. He chased the ball as it bounced down the field, headed right toward the goal. Just as Oliver got there, their goalkeeper came out and grabbed it. Without waiting a second, he held the ball up to kick it down the field. Oliver turned and started to run, afraid the ball was going to hit him.

It did. Right in the rear end.

"Arrrgggggh!" Oliver wailed, falling face-first onto the grass.

But the ball had ricocheted off Oliver's butt. It bounced past the goalkeeper and rolled very slowly toward the goal.

The goalkeeper scrambled to get it, but it was too late. The ball trickled into the goal and stopped before it reached the back of the net.

The ref gave a long blow on his whistle. "Goal!" he yelled. "Halftime!"

I was the first Pirate to realize what had happened. Not even Oliver knew.

"Goal! Goal!" I yelled. I ran toward Oliver but he ran away from me, afraid of being tackled. Everybody on our team started to chase him and he ran around in circles, trying to get away from us.

"What a joke!" Jaden yelled at me as he walked off the field.

Mr. Carmody called us over in a circle. "Listen, boys," he said, "we were lucky. But we were lucky because we were where we were supposed to be. Oliver ran all the way down the field, faster than I've ever seen him run. If you hustle, good things happen. Okay, now drink some water and catch your breath."

I looked at Oliver. He was smiling like he'd won the World Cup.

As I was picking up my water bottle, Mom came over holding a T-shirt. "I don't know where your jersey is, Charlie," she said. "I looked all over. This one is red and it will have to do."

It was my *Buck Meson—Detective from Andromeda* T-shirt. It had a picture on the front of my favorite superhero saying "I DON'T THINK SO!" in big letters. That's what he always says when he's about to

destroy the plans of some evil supervillain.

I put it on. Tommy saw it. "Awesome!" he yelled.

"I don't think so!" he began to chant. "I don't think so! I don't think so! Arrrrr!"

Pretty soon the whole team joined in. All the Pirates together, fighting the evil forces of the universe.

Until Mr. Carmody told us to calm down. He told me to turn the T-shirt inside out, so I did.

But we whispered our chant through the whole halftime.

Just before the game was about to start again, Mr. Carmody clapped his hands. "Okay, guys," he said, "Same lineup as the beginning of the game, except Charlie at forward instead of Vijay." He smiled at me. I saw his eyebrows go up and down.

Holy moly! This was it! Tommy Kasten, Hector Adélia, and Charlie Bumpers on the field at the same time! The Pirates of Doom! We looked at each other and grinned. We were all thinking the same thing.

The Banana.

21

Banana!

The Tigers kicked off and passed the ball down toward our goal. Hector and I stopped at the center line, staying in position and watching what happened. The Pirates defenders were packed in, and every time someone from the Tigers got the ball, one of our teammates met him, trying to slow him down.

When a Tigers forward tried to pass the ball, Sebastian stepped in front of the goal, caught it, and gave it a huge kick. Another Tiger tried to trap it, but he missed. The ball bounced right to Hector, who stopped it on his chest, trapped it, then took off down the middle of the field.

It was time for our play.

"Banana!" I yelled. "Banana!"

The Tigers defenders, including Jaden, were already back, waiting for us. Hector passed me the ball, then headed toward the left side. The defender on Hector followed him from one side of the field to the other. Tommy came running down the left-hand side ahead of the midfielder following him. As I passed it to Tommy, Hector looped behind me like the curve of the world's most beautiful, gigantic banana. I drifted to the right. Jaden, who had been guarding me, ran right into the defender who was trying to stay with Hector. They tripped over each other and fell. I was free on the right side of the goal.

And so was Hector.

The goalkeeper saw I was open and took a half step toward me. At the last second he saw Hector standing all alone in the middle of the penalty box. The goalkeeper froze, then turned to Tommy, who was dribbling straight toward him.

Tommy made a quick pass to Hector, who tapped the ball in.

"Goal!" said the referee.

Parents went crazy.

Tommy fell over and rolled around on the ground. I held up my arms. Hector shrugged and smiled.

Oliver ran in from the sidelines and tackled Hector. So did everyone else.

We were winning! Against the Tigers!

The ref blew the whistle. "This game's not over, players! Line up for the kickoff."

We were lining up when the Tigers coach called the ref over. They talked for a while, then the ref came over to me. "You have to have a real jersey," he said. "You can't wear that shirt."

"I can't find

my jersey," I told him. "But this one is red."

The ref looked back at the other coach, who had his hands on his hips and was shaking his head.

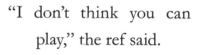

"I don't think you can play," the ref said.

I saw Mr. Carmody coming out onto the field. "What's going on?" he asked.

"This isn't a team jersey." The ref nodded toward the other coach, who was walking over to us. "There's no number."

"Rules are rules," the Tigers coach said. "We let him get away with it for the whole first half, but enough is enough."

Mr. Carmody looked at me. "Charlie," he said, "go stand on the sidelines while we talk about this."

They talked for a long time. The other coach

kept shaking his head, and you could tell that the ref didn't know what to do. He was just a high-school kid, and the ones arguing were grown-ups. Finally Mr. Carmody came over to me where I was standing. "Danny," he said, "go in for Charlie." Danny ran onto the field and Mr. Carmody put his arm around my shoulder.

"Charlie," he said, "You just sit tight and I'll figure out how to get you back in this game."

The parents on our team started yelling. I was pretty mad myself, but it didn't help that the parents were yelling. The ref quieted everyone down and started the game again.

After that it seemed like we couldn't keep the ball on our end of the field and the Tigers were always down near our goal.

The Tigers had two shots that almost went in, but both times the ball hit a side post and bounced away. I could tell it was only a matter of time before they scored. Finally, their biggest player ran over Billy and kicked the ball past Sebastian for an easy goal.

Now it was tied. Two to two.

With no one keeping score.

I wished I could go back in with Tommy and Hector. I just knew the Pirates of Doom could score again.

A few minutes later the Tigers had control of the ball on our side of the field. Sebastian, still playing goalkeeper, looked tired and really nervous. He was screaming at other kids on our team, telling them what to do. You could tell he was frustrated and felt really bad about letting the goal in. Tess kept trying to calm her brother down from the sidelines, but it wasn't working.

I knew how Sebastian felt.

Trevor ran up to me. "Charlie," he said, pulling off his shirt. "Wear this so you can play."

"No," I said. "That's okay. Put it back on. You might have to go in again."

I went over and stood by our coach. "Mr. Carmody?"

He was busy watching so he didn't hear me.

"Mr. Carmody," I repeated. "Let me play goalkeeper. I'll sub for Sebastian."

Coach looked down at me, his eyebrows moving up and down. A smile broke out on his face. "Of course, Charlie! You're a genius."

The next time the ball went out of bounds, Mr. Carmody shouted out for a substitution. I ran onto the field.

"Hey!" the other coach yelled. "He doesn't have the right shirt!"

"Sub for goalkeeper," Mr. Carmody told the ref. "He'll wear the yellow jersey."

Sebastian came running out, pulling off his jersey. "Good luck, Charlie," he said, handing it to me.

Mr. Carmody rearranged everybody on the field. Hector went back up front with Danny. He put Oliver in the midfield with Tommy. Trevor came in as defender along with Boom-Boom.

"You know what to do, boys!" Mr. Carmody called. "It's up to you."

I heard the Squid's voice. "Go, Charlie!" she screeched. "Don't let him hit you in the stomach!"

Ginger barked.

"Hey, Trevor," I said as I ran toward the goal. "Don't get too far away from me. I need you here."

Trevor nodded and smiled a nervous smile.

When play started again, the Tigers brought the ball in on the right side, then tried to work it into the middle. Jaden, playing midfielder now, stopped right in the center of the field. His friend Jack Browning kept trying to dribble the ball by Trevor or Dominic. He wasn't looking to pass—he wanted to score. But every time Jack got it past one of them, the other one always seemed to be there. Everybody was packed in our end of the field, even the defenders from the other team. Every time the ball came to me, I rolled it out to one of my teammates, calling his name, but one of the Tigers always managed to steal it. They were big and there was a lot of pushing, but the ref wasn't calling any fouls. The adults were yelling a lot on the sidelines.

I could feel the pressure. I tried to focus on the ball, but at the same time I kept an eye on Trevor, trying to keep him in position.

The ball went across the midline and one of their defenders gave it a huge kick.

I mean *really* huge.

It went way up in the air and everybody turned to watch it. Two of their players ran in that direction.

The ball was headed right toward Trevor.

"Trevor!" I shouted. "Your ball!"

He glanced over at me for a split second, looking like a scared little prehistoric bunny. Then he looked back up at the ball, braced himself, and stuck his chest out to try and trap the ball. His arms were bent up at his sides like little bird wings. Or maybe Tyrannosaurus rex arms.

"Aaaaaaah!" he screamed. He sounded like a ferocious raptor, attacking its prey.

The ball hit his chest and bounced back the other way. Trevor collapsed on the ground, but the ball arced over three Tigers, bounced up again, then landed right in front of Hector at midfield. He trapped it with his foot, turned, and took off. Everybody was out of position, thinking the Tigers were going to score. Trevor was lying on the ground, probably wondering if he was still alive.

With Hector tearing down the field, Danny took one wing and Tommy took the other. Before I knew it, everyone on our team was chasing them, too. Including Dominic. Only Trevor was left, and he was still lying on the ground.

"Dominic!" I yelled. "Position!"

Boom-Boom didn't hear. Up on the other end of the field I could see Hector pass the ball off to Danny on the left and break for the goal. Tommy was closing in from the right. Danny passed it back to the center. The ball bounced past Hector, headed directly at Tommy.

We were going to score!

And then their goalkeeper stepped in between Tommy and the ball and caught it. Without stopping, he booted it down the field. It landed at midfield, right in front of Jaden. He stopped it and headed toward our goal.

Trevor was just starting to get up.

"Trevor!" I yelled. He looked around like he was wondering what planet he was on.

It was just me and Jaden. Everybody else was far behind, running to catch up, but he wasn't waiting. He dribbled the ball down the field, right toward me. I came out of the goal a little, trying to remember

everything Tess had taught me. My stomach was jumping around and I felt a little dizzy.

Then I heard someone scream, "Ginger, no!"

I knew that voice.

It was the Squid.

Something caught my eye. Ginger was streaking across the field, dragging her leash. She was flying like a heat-seeking rocket.

Right toward her enemy. The soccer ball.

22

Not Going to Lose

Jaden had no idea what was happening until Ginger swept in front of him and attacked the ball. She growled and tried to bite it, pushing it with her nose. Jaden stumbled and almost fell over, but then he just stopped, not sure what to do. Ginger pounced on the ball, looked at Jaden, wondering why he wasn't trying to get the ball back. I ran over and picked up the ball. Ginger wagged her tail and barked, waiting for me to put it down and play with her.

The ref blew the whistle, then ran over and took the ball. The coach from the other team came running out on the field, waving his clipboard.

The grown-ups had lost their minds, screaming and yelling. The players on the other team were stomping around. The Squid was holding her hands in front of her mouth while Mom was talking to her.

Matt was filming.

Dad came out onto the field, grabbed the leash, and pulled Ginger off the field.

Mr. Carmody, the ref, and the other coach talked for a long time. While I stood there watching, the rest of the team gathered around me.

"That was hilarious," Tommy said.

"Yeah," I said. "But I think we're in trouble."

Hector grinned. "What can they do? We don't keep score!"

The ref blew the whistle and held up the ball. "Penalty kick!" He pointed at Jaden. "You're taking it."

The Tigers cheered. So did their parents.

Tess and Mr. Carmody came over to me. "Okay, Charlie," the coach said, "just stay on your toes and do the best you can."

I looked at Jaden, trying to figure out which way he might kick the ball.

"Charlie," Tess said, "don't try to guess. Stay in the center unless you can see which way he's really going. Sometimes you can tell by how he plants his foot. But mostly, just watch and try to feel it."

I nodded. I wanted to be ready to dive for the ball. But what if I guessed wrong? Then I would look ridiculous.

As the ref put the ball down for Jaden to kick, I felt like I was in another world. People were yelling, but they seemed a million miles away.

Jaden stood back from the ball. He looked nervous, too. We were both freaking out!

The ref blew the whistle. Jaden looked at me, took a deep breath, then took three big steps forward. I watched him come up to the ball and focused on where he planted his foot.

Bam!

In a split second, I saw the ball was hurtling right at me.

We were *not* going to lose another game! I stepped up.

Ooof! The ball smacked me right in the stomach. It knocked the breath out of me, but I wrapped my arms around it and held on tight.

I fell on top of the ball and lay there trying to breathe.

Before I could move, a bunch of kids piled on top of me. All the Pirates. Even Victor.

"Get in position, Pirates!" Mr. Carmody shouted. "The game's not over!"

I stood in front of the goal while the others took their places on the field. But as soon as I passed the ball to Dominic, the ref blew the whistle. "Time!"

The game was over.

It was a tie.

Though no one was keeping score.

"Line up, line up!" Mr. Carmody yelled. We went down the line, shaking hands with the Tigers. A couple of the fifth graders looked like they were about to cry.

Including Jaden.

I guess it was hard not to win against a bunch of puny fourth-grade pirates.

"Nice stop, son," their coach said to me.

Mr. Carmody called us to gather around him. "I have never been prouder than I am right now," he told us. "You all played your best today, using the skills we have practiced all season. Well done, team! And let's give a big hand to the player who attacked the ball like a dinosaur—Trevor!"

We all cheered and clapped. Trevor had a grin on his face I didn't think would ever come off.

"And I also want to recognize Charlie. He stepped up and volunteered to play goalkeeper even though he would've rather played somewhere else. And look what he did!"

"Char-lie! Char-lie! Char-lie!" everyone chanted.

Mr. Carmody beamed at me. That felt pretty good.

"And finally," he said, "how about our new defender, Ginger?"

162

A couple of guys started barking and everybody laughed.

"We'll be in touch about the pizza party for all the players and their families," Coach Carmody said. "Thanks for all your hard work."

Then Mrs. Patel shouted, "All of you who still have candy bars and money, please see me before you leave! It's really important. And it looks like Oliver is going to win the prize."

Everybody cheered again. Except for me.

The candy bars. I'd forgotten all about the candy bars!

23

¡Qué horrible!

In a flash, I wasn't thinking about the good game we'd played anymore. We were short almost $100! Where were we going to get that much money?

While everybody else said goodbye, Tommy, Hector, and I walked over to Mrs. Patel.

"Here to settle things up?" she asked.

I looked at my two friends. I figured Hector wasn't going to talk. He was the quiet one. I could tell by the terrified look on Tommy's face that he wasn't going to say anything either.

That left me to explain. "Mrs. Patel," I said. "We've got a problem."

She frowned. "What is it?"

"Um, it's sort of complicated. We did sell a lot of candy bars and collect a bunch of money, but, well…"

"We ate some of the candy," said Tommy.

"And," added Hector, "we didn't write everything down at first."

"The worst part is, I lost some of the money on the bus. In other words, we owe you around $100 and we have to figure out how to make it back."

"Hmmm," she said, crossing her arms over her chest. "This is a problem, all right. Should we talk to your parents about it?"

I looked at Tommy. I could tell he hadn't said anything to his parents. And I didn't know about Hector.

"Okay," I mumbled.

"Let's go talk to them now," Mrs. Patel said. "They're right over there."

We all turned to look. Tommy's parents, Hector's parents, and Mom and Dad were all standing around in a circle, talking.

That many parents talking at once is never a good thing.

Mrs. Patel headed toward the circle of parents. "You boys stay right here for a minute," she said.

Tommy, Hector, and I watched her shake hands with everyone. Then they started talking.

"This is really bad," Tommy said.

"You're right," I said.

"*¡Qué horrible!*" Hector moaned.

Our parents kept glancing over at us. Tommy's dad was doing a lot of the talking. After a while they all nodded and laughed.

"This definitely does not look good," Tommy said. "When my dad laughs like that, he's usually planning something evil."

My dad motioned all of us over. We walked— very slowly.

"It sounds like you boys are pretty deep in debt," Tommy's dad said.

We all nodded.

"You know that means you owe a lot of money?" Mr. Adélia asked.

We nodded again.

"You should have told us you were having trouble," my mom said.

We nodded again.

"When I was a kid," my dad said, "my father used to say 'One boy has a brain, two boys together each have half a brain, and three boys together have lost their minds.'"

Ha ha ha, I thought.

"We've talked it over," Mrs. Kasten said. "We'll cover the cost of the candy bars."

Omigosh! What a huge relief! I loved parents! I tried not to smile, and I could tell Tommy and Hector were doing the same.

"But...," my dad said, then paused.

Uh-oh. I didn't like that pause.

"You'll have to earn the money back," he went on. "And we have some work for you."

That seemed okay.

"I have a special crew in my parks and recreation work," Tommy's dad said.

"Oh no," Tommy muttered under his breath. "Not that."

"For the next four Saturdays you'll be helping them in the dog parks," Mr. Kasten said.

Mrs. Adélia covered her mouth to keep from laughing. Mr. Adélia smiled and cleaned off his glasses. All the other parents were grinning ear to ear. So was Mrs. Patel.

"B-but…," Tommy stammered.

"We don't…" I couldn't think of anything to say.

"Then we'll be all even," Mr. Kasten declared. "Is it a deal?"

Tommy, Hector, and I looked at each other. "Okay," we all said.

"Fine," said Mr. Kasten. "That's settled."

"*¡Qué horrible!*" I said.

Our parents laughed.

24

Transformation

Tommy and Hector came over in the afternoon and we kicked the ball around the yard for a while, trying to keep it away from Ginger. Dad ordered pizza for dinner, and when it got there we all went in and sat at the kitchen table.

"Where's Matt?" asked Mom. She went to the bottom of the stairs and called for him.

He didn't answer.

"Charlie, will you run upstairs and get him?"

I raced up to Matt's room. The door was closed, so I knocked. No answer. I figured he had his headphones on. I pounded more.

"Go away!" he yelled.

"Dinner's ready. It's pizza."

"I'm busy," he said.

Matt never turned down pizza. Now I was really curious. "Can I come in?"

"No way. Get lost."

"What are you doing?"

"Go away," he said.

I headed back downstairs. "He's busy," I said to everyone. "He doesn't want to be bothered."

But Mom saved Matt three slices of pizza anyway. As we finished, he came downstairs holding his computer.

"Everybody in the family room, please," he said. "You are invited to attend the premiere of a future classic."

"What's it about?" Tommy asked. He and Matt got along pretty well. I guess maybe I would get along with Matt, too, if he weren't my older brother.

"It's about you guys."

"Stupific!" Tommy said.

"I don't want to see it," I said. "It just makes fun of us."

"Keep your pants on," Matt said.

"My pants *are* on."

I followed them into the family room and sat down. Matt hooked up his computer to the television and turned on the video.

Pulsing music started to play and a title appeared on the screen: THE SAGA OF CHARLIE BUMPERS AND THE PUNY PIRATES.

"I'm not watching this." But even though I knew it would be a nightmare, I couldn't help looking.

"Just wait," Matt said.

"This had better be good, Matt," Dad warned.

"Why doesn't anybody trust me?" my brother asked.

We watched one scene after another of our soccer season, the first goal that was scored against us by the Tigers, Oliver and Victor standing in the middle of the field talking, Trevor running away from the ball, different views of Pirates falling over. And in between all that we saw shot after shot of the other teams scoring goals. The music underneath it was like something from a movie when the Dark Lords of Whatever were conquering the world.

It was terrible. "This isn't funny," I said.

Then another title screen appeared.

SOMETIMES THEY SCORED.

The first scene showed the other team kicking it into their own goal by mistake. And then four more goals being scored on us.

"Ha ha ha," I said.

"People scored a million goals on us!" Tommy yelled. He didn't seem bothered. Hector had his head in his hands.

Then another title came up on the screen:
TRANSFORMATION.

"What's that mean?" asked the Squid.

"It means something is changing," Mom said with a smile.

The video showed Hector scoring one of our first goals. It continued with two more Pirate goals. And then it showed Dominic kicking the ball out of our end of the field over and over again.

Every now and then there were pictures of Mr. Carmody encouraging us. And a lot of shots of Tess talking to us. A whole lot of shots of Tess.

"Hmmmm." Dad gave Matt a little smile.

"Stop it," Matt said.

But we kept watching. We saw Pirates passing to one another. Pirates during practice, doing drills. Trevor screaming like a raptor. I didn't know Matt had filmed us that much.

Then it showed the Pirates of Doom—Tommy, Hector, and me.

"The Banana!" Tommy, Hector, and I yelled.

"This is great!" Tommy said.

The Squid appeared on the screen, cheering from the sidelines. "There's me!" she squealed.

Then I appeared in the yellow shirt. I recognized the play right away. It was the game against the Cougars, that time I got hit in the stomach and dropped the ball.

"Not this!" I groaned.

But just as I came up to meet the attacking player and stopped the ball, it cut to another scene. I was surprised—I thought Matt would show the Cougars scoring.

After that came a whole string of quick shots of me stopping one ball after another, calling to teammates, and rolling the ball out to them. I had no idea that had happened so many times.

And then it cut to Ginger chasing the ball. She attacked it in slow motion, taking it away from Jaden. We all cracked up. Ginger jumped up and barked at the screen.

And finally, we came to the penalty kick. The video showed Tess, calming me down.

"There's that girl again," the Squid observed. "She's always there."

Matt didn't say anything. I kept watching the screen. As Jaden stood behind the ball and ran up to kick it, the movie went into slow motion, with big, loud music like they would play in the Olympics. It showed me catching the ball. You could see the air blowing out of my mouth and the wide-eyed look on my face. And everyone running up and piling on me.

"*¡Maravillosa!*" Hector yelled.

"Right!" we all agreed.

The screen showed another title—THE PUNY PIRATES. Slowly the word PUNY morphed into PESKY, then into POWERFUL.

We all applauded. Matt clicked off his laptop and the TV went black.

"So why doesn't anyone ever trust me?" Matt asked.

"I do," Tommy said.

"So do I," Hector said.

"Me too," I said.

"Really?" Matt asked.

I smiled. "Kind of."

"Was it a tie?" the Squid asked.

"We don't know," I said, smiling.

"Why not?" she asked.

Tommy, Hector, and I looked at each other. We were the Pirates of Doom, and we all answered together.

"Because no one was keeping score! ARRRRR!"

Don't miss the other books
in the Charlie Bumpers series—
Charlie Bumpers vs. the Teacher of the Year,
Charlie Bumpers vs. the Really Nice Gnome,
Charlie Bumpers vs. the Squeaking Skull, and
Charlie Bumpers vs. the Perfect Little Turkey.

Also available as audio books.

HC: 978-1-56145-732-8
PB: 978-1-56145-824-0
CD: 978-1-56145-770-0

HC: 978-1-56145-835-6
PB: 978-1-56145-963-6
CD: 978-1-56145-893-6

HC: 978-1-56145-740-3
PB: 978-1-56145-831-8
CD: 978-1-56145-788-5

HC: 978-1-56145-808-0
PB: 978-1-56145-888-2
CD: 978-1-56145-809-7

And watch for the sixth book
in the series, coming up soon!

BILL HARLEY is the author of the award-winning middle reader novels *The Amazing Flight of Darius Frobisher* and *Night of the Spadefoot Toads*. He is also a storyteller, musician, and writer who has been writing and performing for kids and families for more than twenty years. Harley is the recipient of Parents' Choice and ALA awards, as well as two Grammy Awards. He lives in Massachusetts.

www.billharley.com

ADAM GUSTAVSON has illustrated many books for children, including *Lost and Found*; *The Blue House Dog*; *Mind Your Manners, Alice Roosevelt!*; and *Snow Day!* He lives in New Jersey.

www.adamgustavson.com